I0519962

Greenwoman
A Literary Garden of . . .
Fiction * Nonfiction * Poetry * Commentary
Biography *Art * Comics

Volume 1 - Germination

Editor-In-Chief: Sandra Knauf
Deputy Editor: Zora Knauf
Copy Editor: Cheri Colburn

Chief Designer: Sandra Knauf
Art Director: Rachael Kloster
Web Designer/Tech. Support: Paul Spielman

For advertising contact:
Sandra Knauf
(719) 473-9237
sandra@greenwomanmagazine.com

Greenwoman Publishing, LLC
P. O. Box 6587, Colo. Spgs., CO
80934-6587

Attn. retailers: For more information about
selling this marvelous publication in your
store call (719) 473-9237 or write
sandra@greenwomanmagazine.com

Copyright 2011, 2014
Greenwoman Publications, LLC. All rights
reserved. Reproduction in whole or in part
without permission is prohibited.

ISBN-10: 0989705641
ISBN-13: 978-0-9897056-4-6

www.greenwomanmagazine.com
www.florasforum.com
www.zeraandthegreenman.com
www.greenwomanpublishing.com

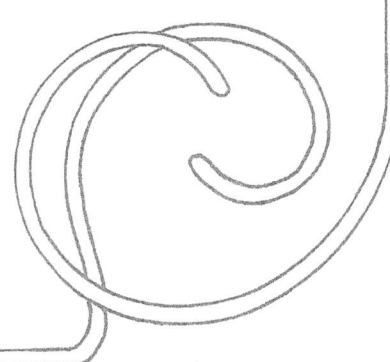

Contents

Front cover art by Sandra Knauf and Paul Spielman, with
Zora Knauf, Ethan Burke, and "Mrs. Raccoon" at the
Vermijo Community Garden, Colorado Springs,
Colorado, August 2010.

Back cover art, *Tree of Feminine Thought*,
by Jane Schwartz Gates.

Seeds of Change collage reprinted from *The Ex-Urban-
ite's Complete and Illustrated Easy-Does-It First Time
Farmer's Guide*, with permission from Wendy Kaysing.

Editor's Letter

Welcome to our garden!

I started this publication for one reason—I believe in the transformative power of connecting with nature. Like most of you, I make this connection through gardening. Through gardening I explore the life that soil is and soil creates (our sustenance), I interact with garden creatures great and small, I participate in the miraculous by planting seeds that create beauty, food, wonder. All of these activities nourish the mind, body, and heart.

Great garden writing explores these connections, as well as the ways gardening relates to science, fashion, politics, history, spirituality, relationships—*everything*. It gives voice to this transformative power.

This first volume is very special. The contributors found in these pages have allowed me to publish their work knowing that this is an independent venture with almost no starting capital. I would like to thank all of you again for your kindness and generosity.

I also want to thank my brilliant daughter, Zora, for acting as my indispensible right-hand woman. Among her numerous qualities, she is one of the most capable people I have ever met.

Just days ago I received word that I have been awarded a grant from Pikes Peak Community Foundation to help with costs through this first year. I would like to acknowledge their generosity. I am filled with gratitude at yet another sign that I am on the right path—that this endeavor is meant to be.

In these pages I hope to dazzle you with the wonderment that is garden writing. I hope that you will love this publication as much as I do.

Sandra

Sandra Knauf
Editor and Publisher

Zora Knauf,
Deputy Editor
Extraordinaire

Contributors

Kristian Angel is a community volunteer, military wife, working mom, artist, and activist. Her volunteer work includes being the Founder and Executive Director of Greenville, South Carolina's NORML, a precinct president for Greenville GOP, and work at the local children's shelter.

Cheryl Conklin (a "Leafing Through" book reviewer) is a life-long gardener and writer who somehow managed to fold these passions into past careers in theatre, teaching, and counseling and to synthesize a mousse worth living.

Rachael Davis says, "I consider it fate when I met [editor] Sandra at a start-up meeting for a downtown organic and local farmer's market Colorado Springs last year." They've been collaborating and swapping stories on gardening adventures, children, and creative work ever since. Rachael's mixed media art has been shown in Colorado. She holds a BFA from the Kansas City Art Institute and is now pursuing a MFA in Fort Collins, Colorado.

When **Joyce Deming** (a "Leafing Through" book reviewer) is not hiking in Colorado's high country or working in her garden, she likes to foist her favorite books and authors on the unsuspecting public at the Jefferson County Public Library where she works as a librarian. She and her husband share a small farm east of Golden with three cats, three sheep, five ducks, and the world's smartest border collie. You can read more of her book suggestions at: http://jeffcolibrary.org/booklovers/choice.html.

D'Arcy Fallon is an award-winning journalist who has been a staff writer for such publications as the *Long Beach Press-Telegram*, the *San Francisco Examiner*, and the *Colorado Springs Gazette*. She is the author of a memoir, *So Late, So Soon*, about living in a religious commune in the early 70s. She teaches journalism and creative writing at Wittenberg University in Springfield, Ohio. She has a thing for garlic, border collies, and peonies. dfallon@wittenberg.edu.

Maureen Fry lives on a lovely 150-acre organic farm/nature preserve in Champaign County, Ohio. Her poetry has appeared in a number of journals; her poem, "The Way It Is," was nominated for a Pushcart Prize. She retired in 2009 from a 30-year career at Wittenberg University, where she was director of the Writing Center and taught a variety of writing courses and seminars.

Kim Gravestock's garden design work (she's the owner of From the Ground Up) can be seen at The Cliffhouse, a five-star hotel in Manitou Springs, Colorado. Over the last fifteen years, she's been a beekeeper, a Beekeeping School Coordinator, and Vice President for the Pikes Peak Beekeeping Association. She's shared her extensive horticultural know-how as a featured speaker at the Pikes Peak Landscape Symposium, as an instructor for the CSU Master Gardener program, and through tours of her garden. Photographing plants, bugs and other wonders of Nature is her latest endeavor.

Contributors

Pat Cook Gulya recently retired from a technology career and city life. She currently gardens on a large rural plot , growing a wide variety of vegetables, flowers and trees. She bicycles to keep in shape for summer touring in the Colorado mountains, practices and teaches yoga, and writes essays and fiction. Her writing has appeared in the *Colorado Springs Gazette* column "That's Life," and aired on KRCC's "Western Skies."
http://www.dancingheartsstudio.com/blog/

Elisabeth Kinsey (our "Sex in the Garden" columnist) teaches writing online, lives in New York, pines away for Half Moon Bay and publishes in *The Denver Post* and various journals. Her hands are imminently dirty. She may or may not be related to the late Dr. Alfred Kinsey.

Bill McDorman is President of Seeds Trust (High Altitude Gardens), founded in 1984. He has over 30 years experience in the bioregional seed business and has started three seed companies and two non-profits. He is the Executive Director of Native Seeds/S.E.A.R.C.H. in Tucson, Arizona and author of *Basic Seed Saving*.

Dan Murphy (our "Slow Ride" columnist) is a seasoned zine writer (*The Juniper, Elephant Mess*) and proponent of the slow life. His long-time passions include bike riding, skateboarding, punk rock, and gardening. His new interests include botany, ecology, wildflowers, and lichens. Dan has a B.S. in horticulture and is currently in Illinois pursuing an M.S. in biology. His thesis is on green roof technology research. http://www.juniperbug.blogspot.com

Bruce Holland Rogers was born in dry, dry Tucson, Arizona, and now lives in wet, wet Eugene, Oregon. He enjoys the prospect of gardening but doesn't much like the actual work. If not for Holly, his wife, he would never have any home-grown tomatoes. Rogers teaches fiction writing in the MFA program of the Northwest Institute of Literary Arts.
http://www.shortshortshort.com

DB Rudin (our "The Creature Feature" columnist) is an environmental education consultant, elementary school teacher, and the Education Coordinator at Venetucci Farm, an 190-acre historic farm in Colorado Springs, Colorado. He offers programs through Colorado Critter Encounters, which includes hands-on programs for kids on nature and conservation, and a class for those who tend the soil, The Good, the Bad and the Beautiful: Bugs 101 for Gardeners.
http://www.cocritterencounters.com

Jane Schwartz Gates is a painter, illustrator, writer, and landscape designer. Her work centers around the connectedness of all life in Nature and power of the female spirit. She lives in California. You can see more at her websites www.janeschwartzgatesart.com and http://www.gardengates.info.

Contributors

Eva Syrovy is an immigrant from the Czech Republic who has been a daughter and mother (two boys, one grown), an oil field "frack rat," a teacher, a diligent runner and cyclist, a lazy gardener, a decent cook and quilter, and a lousy housekeeper. Her writing, about the kids she mothers and teaches, history, and the environment, has been most regularly published in the *Colorado Springs Business Journal* and *The Denver Post*.

Ana Maria Spagna lives, writes, and gardens in Stehekin, Washington, a remote valley in the North Cascades accessible only by foot, boat, boat or float plane. Her books include *Now Go Home: Wilderness, Belonging, and the Crosscut Saw*, named a *Seattle Times* Best Book of 2004, *Test Ride on the Sunnyland Bus: A Daughter's Civil Rights Journey*, winner of the 2009 *River Teeth* Literary Nonfiction Prize, and the forthcoming essay collection *Potluck: Community at the Edge of Wilderness*.

Michael A. Stusser is a Seattle-based freelance writer and game inventor. His first book, *The Dead Guy Interviews: Conversations with 45 of the Most Accomplished, Notorious, and Deceased Personalities in History* (Penguin Publishing) was released to critical acclaim in 2008. Stusser is a columnist for mental_floss magazine and his work is frequently published by *Yoga International*, *Seattle Weekly*, and the *New York Times Syndicate*.

Stephen C. Thomas is an itinerant writer originally from Atlanta. He is a contributing editor for RealitySandwich.com, where he covers the environment, culture and consciousness as ST Frequency.

Carolyne Wright has published eight books and chapbooks of poetry, four collections of poetry, and a volume of essays. Her most recent collections are *A Change of Maps* (Lost Horse Press, 2006), and *Seasons of Mangoes and Brainfire* (Carnegie Mellon UP/ EWUP-Lynx House Books, 2nd edition 2005). A poem of hers appears in The Best American Poetry 2009, and in *The Pushcart Prize XXXIV: Best of the Small Presses* (2010). A native of Seattle, she teaches for the Northwest Institute of Literary Arts' Whidbey Writers Workshop MFA program.

Informed Simplicity

Life is expensive. Humans consume considerable amounts of resources daily (especially North Americans). Some of this consumption is necessary for survival, but most is excess, which ultimately ends up in our landfills and junkyards. Much of what we consume and waste can be given a monetary value, but the cost of extracting these materials cannot so easily be assessed. Forests are cleared, water and air polluted, ecosystems spoiled. Can you put a dollar amount on a wetland or a mountain? What is the value of a rare plant species? The true cost of life is incalculable.

The natural world relies on nutrient cycles and energy flow to function properly. Where there is a break in the energy flow or a dearth in nutrients, tragedy often ensues. Conventional farming is a prime example. As crops grow, they mine the soil for nutrients. In the natural world, these nutrients would be replaced as plants and animals die. In an agricultural setting, plants are often completely removed, and this feedback portion of the nutrient cycle is lost. In order to compensate, farmers must add copious amounts of fertilizer (usually synthetic) to achieve high yields. Removal of the plant layer also leaves the soil unprotected, leading to erosion and additional nutrient loss. In this case, a better understanding of ecological principles combined with sustainable practices would lead to a healthier agricultural system.

So, why am I giving you this lecture about the cost of living and the value of properly functioning nutrient and energy cycles? Well, I'm trying to make an argument for simple and mindful living. These days we are being inundated with "green" propaganda. While once relegated to the fringes of society, the green movement has now been co-opted by the mainstream, and whether they are in it for the money or because they really care, it doesn't change the fact that the message has become ubiquitous. But is it convincing? Frankly, most mainstream arguments seem vague and untenable, and their solutions are often equally questionable (e.g. don't buy less stuff, just buy different stuff). So, I don't know how well the campaign is working or how long it will last. Are people getting sick of hearing it? Are they seeing it for the corporate greenwashing that it very well may be? Does anybody even care?

SLOW Ride by
Dan Murphy

Of course people care. Nobody wants to see the planet go down the crapper. Most people want to do the right thing. The problem isn't that people are ambivalent; it's that they are ignorant. It's one thing to tell people what to do. It's another to help them understand why they should do it. If the general public were more environmentally educated and ecologically minded, encouraging them to mend their fuelish ways would be much easier. If the masses had a basic understanding about the importance of biodiversity and the services that ecosystems offer us when they are functioning properly, living green would come more naturally. Eco-literacy makes for a more eco-minded society, and an eco-minded society is a sustainable one.

So, how do we become more eco-literate? As with any new concept, it's best to start small and simple. Spend some time outside in nature. Learn the names of the plants and animals that are common in your area. Grow native plants in your garden. Visit your local watershed. Research the environmental issues that impact your region and find out what you can do about them. Volunteer with a local organization that does environmental work. Ask questions. Participate in workshops. Most importantly, don't just accept everything that is placed in front of you by the media. Find out for yourself if what you've heard about an environmental product or issue is credible. Being skeptical isn't the same as being cynical. Skepticism is science, and it is through critical thinking and scientific research that answers are realized. Good science (i.e., empirical evidence) allows us to move forward with greater knowledge and understanding. As a citizen scientist, you will be part of a global movement to better understand our home planet, and with that greater understanding, you will become a more effective steward.

I am a proponent of the simple life. I am by no means the paragon of such a lifestyle, but I'm working at it. Along the way I have found that living simply requires, among other things, patience, conviction and intelligence. Living small means living smart. If you want to avoid getting ripped off, it helps to be an informed consumer. If you want to help protect the planet, it helps to be an informed human. So don't let the science scare you, get out into the world and get informed. The planet will thank you. ❀

A Human Birth

by Bruce Holland Rogers

The children. The laundry. The marriage. The dishes. The bounced check. The stained carpet. When it all became too much for Denise, she would leave the apartment in whatever state it was in, however many pots were simmering on the stove, however loudly the kids were arguing, and walk down three flights of stairs to the tiny entryway garden. She would lie behind the diminutive hedge, face down with her nose in the grass, feeling the cool earth under her body, inhaling its scent. She imagined the earth swallowing her up—not to bury her, but to give her a place of refuge. Eventually, her husband would find her, walk her back up to the apartment, and put a cold washcloth on her forehead. He would finish making dinner, clean up, and put the kids to bed. She knew it wasn't fair to him at all. He worked hard, only to come home to this.

One day, as she waited for someone else's wash to finish spinning in the only washing machine that wasn't out of order, a voice behind her said, "Hey, neighbor." She turned. He was tall and wide, the man from down the hall. Bruno? Bart? She couldn't remember.

He stopped short. "Bad day?" he asked.

"A day like all the others," she said.

"Hm," he said. The spin cycle finished. He started pulling out his clothes and loading them in a hamper.

"It's hard, very hard," she said, even though she hardly knew him, this Brent, this Barney. "I just..."

As he wheeled his clothes to the dryer he glanced at her to show that he was listening.

"It's hard being a human being."

He stopped what he was doing, stood up tall, and looked at her with interest. "Why would you say that?"

Denise shrugged and started loading the washing machine. "That's how it feels."

Bryan or Burl took a pencil from his pocket and removed an old announcement from the bulletin board. On the back, he wrote Thursday, 7:00, basement of First Christian. He drew a map showing an intersection and the location of the church. "Here." He gave it to her.

"What's this?"

"A weekly meeting. People who understand. Trust me. You'll see."

"I don't know," she said.

Wednesday, the children had a half day at school. They were wild, messy, loud. A mysterious stench came from somewhere under the sink. When Denise opened the refrigerator, she discovered that the milk was warm. Everything was warm. Frozen dinners were melting in the freezer.

She walked down, leaving the children on their own. She lay in the grass, nose to the ground. The earth smelled black and safe. Rich. Chocolate. She even touched the tip of her tongue to the soil. No, not chocolate. It did not taste like chocolate, but it was good.

When her husband came home from work, he collected her from behind the hedge. "Honey," he said, "You need help. You need to talk to someone."

* * *

Thursday night at 6:45, Denise found herself in the church basement. A dozen folding chairs faced one another in a circle. A schedule on the wall noted the meeting times for Alcoholics Anonymous, Overeaters Anonymous, Gamblers Anonymous, and Adult Children of Alcoholics. The schedule didn't say anything about Thursdays at 7:00.

One by one, they came in: the tall narrow man in a green jacket, the brown-eyed woman with a nervous twitch, the fat man whose eyes only opened halfway, the woman with shadows under her eyes. Right before seven, her neighbor came in. He nodded, smiled at her.

"Well, I guess it's about that time," said the fat man.

"I'll start," said the neighbor. "I'm Bjorn."

"Hi, Bjorn," said everyone in the room but Denise.

"I'm managing to avoid places where I know I'll act like a beast. No all-you-can-eat buffets." He patted his belly. "Usually by this time of year, I have loaded on the weight. This year, I'm doing much better. I'm still worried about winter, though. Winter comes, and all I want to do is stay in bed with the blankets over my head. Last year, I used up all my sick leave, and I got fired. I don't want that to happen again. My sponsor told me that I should call him from bed if I can't get up. He'll talk me through it. I hope that works."

When Bjorn finished, the room was silent. Denise wasn't sure what to think. She didn't have a problem with eating too much, or with staying in bed.

"I'm Tina," said the twitchy woman.

"Hi, Tina," said the group.

"When I buy groceries, I can't help myself. I buy more of what we already have. The cupboards at our place are full, but I can't stop buying more canned soup, bags of dry beans." Tina went on to reveal how she hid food under the seats of her car, behind a potted plant in the lobby of her building, out on the fire escape. "I know I should stop. It's hard. I try not to buy another bag of flour, but then I think, What if? What if I can't find the bags I have already hidden?"

The next to speak was Lauren. She had a hard time sleeping at night. Even though she didn't see particularly well in the dark, she remembered a time when she could. She knew it wasn't a safe thing to do, but she often got up while her husband was sleeping and prowled the dark alleys until dawn. She would drag herself through the next day at work, hardly able to keep her eyes open. However, as soon as the sun went down again, it didn't matter. She was wide awake.

"I'm Enrique."

"Hi, Enrique."

"In my past life, I was a boa constrictor..."

Denise sat up straight. Had Enrique just said that he used to be a snake? He looked a little like he could still be one. He was tall and thin. His head swayed at the top of his neck. He explained how he really needed to stay out of bars, that he always found himself getting into fights.

Denise looked across the circle at Tina, who liked to squirrel away food. She looked at Bjorn, who this winter was going to fight the urge to hibernate. Bjorn nodded and gave her a little smile. What nocturnal creature had Lauren been in her past life? A possum? A raccoon?

Crazy, Denise thought, What am I doing here with these people? What in the world?

Illustration by Rachael Davis

Enrique was still talking. He never lost a fight. He always managed to choke the other guy out. "I'm lucky I haven't killed anyone," Enrique said. "That's the worst of bad karma, you know? If I were to kill some guy, I'd have to come back as something really simple and lowly, you know? Something like, I don't know. A worm." The last word hung in the air, smelling of moist earth, the safety of darkness.

With that, Denise hugged herself and began to cry. No one got up and went to her. Apparently, they were used to moments like this.

"I'm..." she started, but then couldn't manage to keep her breathing even. She keened.

"It's all right," someone said. "Take your time."

Someone else passed her a tissue.

When she finally got control over her breathing, she said, "I'm Denise."

"Hi, Denise."

"I just realized that I shouldn't be so hard on myself," she said, wiping her eyes. "I have come so far." ❋

Worm

by Rachael Davis

Growing Locally

by Sandra Knauf

For over a decade I longed to try community gardening. From what I'd read, these gardens were beautiful, creative ways to connect with other gardeners and the ideal way to grow nutritious food in the city. In 1998, our city of 360,000 had three gardens. I joined one but found the numerous rules overwhelming—I couldn't build our young daughters a sunflower house, use pruned branches from our old lilac for pole beans, or grow any other flowers. While others appreciated the structure, I needed more freedom. I didn't last a week.

By 2009 our city had grown to 500,000 but we still had only three community gardens. Enter Pikes Peak Urban Gardens, a nonprofit with a mission to create three or four new gardens every year. I learned about PPUG; their driving interests were sustainability and better health through better food. When I heard that a garden was slated for a vacant lot only eleven blocks away, my heart raced. All the plots were taken, but I got on a waiting list. That growing season dragged on like no other. Then, I got word of another new garden in a nearby park. I was in!

That first year at Vermijo Garden near Fountain Creek proved . . . interesting. The picturesque setting (mountain backdrop, a creek close by) delighted the sixteen of us, but starting from scratch was tough. We had water, good soil (trucked in, as a necessity) and a protective fence, but the underlying ground was road base. Unskilled at carpentry, we struggled building raised beds. We noticed that several homeless souls had made the park their camp site and suspected that some of the park's visitors used the park as a rendezvous for drug deals.

THIS BOY GREW THESE VEGETABLES ON ONE TWENTIETH OF AN ACRE

It wasn't perfect, but we felt it could be. We found strategies to deal with the flea beetles (who feasted on our arugula and radishes) and the harsh June winds. We realized the homeless were not a threat. With more traffic to the area the criminal element decreased. We put up art, donated some of our produce to a church each week and acted as garden hosts and hostesses, proudly showing off our labors during a festival. We had fun and made friends. I grew tomatillos, fava beans, *Rosa Bianca* eggplants, *Black Spanish* radishes, French fingerling potatoes—and flowers—lots of flowers! A friend grew fennel and shared with the swallowtail butterfly larvae. It was very hard work but we were thrilled with our creation.

It's only year two but the garden looks fabulous. This spring we found the soil richer from our fall additions of organic nutrients. Plots are more "together" in thought and structure. Some of us have been taking gardening classes (also courtesy of PPUG) and are more confident in our abilities. A few gardeners didn't stay, but new ones with fresh ideas and energy eagerly joined. Visitors come by every day to admire our efforts and ask questions.

Vermijo Community Garden is now a significant part of our lives and our neighborhood.We turned an unused portion of a park, a rectangle of road base where nothing grew at all, into a mini-oasis of beauty and life.

It's only year three for PPUG, but there are now nearly a dozen community gardens in Colorado Springs. Thank you for helping our city grow. ❋

Gone Native

by Ana Maria Spagna

She fills her pockets and her pack and her shirt and loiters long, too long, until our companions move on up the trail. Miles from here they will check their watches or the angle of the sun through the forest and, if they are in the know, shake their heads. Meanwhile, she slips a papery pod through her calloused fingertips.

"Too green," she says.

Then she tests one more, peeling back the brown transparent husk, veins like parallel pen-and-ink strokes, fine and thin in the silhouette of the light.

"Just right," she says.

She slips it into a baggie, then into side pocket of her Carhartt shorts.

"Take only pictures, leave only footprints," I say.

She shrugs and reaches for the next pod. I set my pack on the ground, retrieve a water bottle and sigh.

Sometimes we carry the *Pojar*. The full title is *Plants of the Pacific Northwest Coast: Washington, Oregon, British Columbia & Alaska*, compiled and edited by Jim Pojar and Andy MacKinnon, but Northwesterners who love native plants call it simply the *Pojar*. Like the Bible. Today's booty is lupine. According to the Pojar, grizzlies favor Nootka lupine, and native tribes ate the roots, pit-cooked despite the fact that it's chock-full of toxic alkaloids. (Don't try this at home!) Blue and

pea-like and ubiquitous, lupine also has roots thick as a forearm and stubborn as a two-year old at bedtime. That last part isn't in the *Pojar*, but I'm here to say it's true. We've tried transplanting. No luck. So now it's the seeds. A neighbor bought fifty pounds of native lupine seed and offered us all we'd like, but she'll have none of it.

"Why not?" I asked.

"I like to collect my own," she said. "It's my hobby."

When she was a child she picked up rocks on the beach, every rock, and cried if she had to leave before she'd gotten them all, her parents say. I've heard diagnoses for this, both psychological and cultural, but I am not going there. She's not obsessed; she's infatuated. She's been seduced by the stripping, the saving, the drying, then planting, then cultivating. Then waiting. Part of the magic is the waiting.

"Can we go now?" I ask.

"Not yet," she says. "In a minute."

At home, seeds stick to her pockets and her socks in the laundry; they overfill baggies, permanent marker labeled, on the radiant heat tiles in the bathroom, and paper sacks in the mud room, and sometimes jars in the freezer: chocolate lily, tiger lily, yarrow, phlox. And not just seeds. Three dozen pots line the side of the house, under the shed eaves to catch the rain. Each is filled with tiny Western red cedars, some not an inch tall, which formerly grew along a trail where they sprouted, five thousand of them, after a fire. She dug some up and packed them out.

Cedar, according to the *Pojar*, was used by natives for canoes, house planks, totem poles, paddles, baskets, clothing, dishes, ceremonial drum logs, and a variety of tools. Non-natives like us use it for shingles, shakes, siding, boats (some things never change), caskets, closets. The leaf oil makes perfumes, insecticides, veterinary soaps, shoe polishes and deodorants. Valuable booty.

"Why'd you take the trees?" I asked.

"They'd be cleared eventually," she argued. "They didn't stand a chance."

She should know. She started her life in the woods on a trail crew. Back then, she'd stop mid-work, tool in hand, while clearing brush from a trail into which wild-flowers intruded, to strip the pods. Rescue, it was, pure and simple.

I tried this reasoning once in a distant national park.

"Could I have just this one seedling, please, the one that's growing in silt in the culvert?" I asked.

The ranger stared.

"It will be cleared eventually," I said.

"If you don't want a ticket," the ranger said, "you can buy one in the visitor center for thirty bucks."

Out of town guests, coerced into an innocent hike with her, are likely to be corrupted straight away. Her brother once collected a baggie-full of red columbine seed. (The Quileute, according to the *Pojar*, chewed columbine leaves and spat them on sores. We do not.) He was sheepish and uncertain, not one for civil disobedience. But her passion is hard to resist, so he took them home to Seattle where he stuck them in pots in his garage and waited. Three years later, at his wedding reception, a small pot with a wildflower seedling sat at each guest's table: the bounty from that trip. He and his new wife had found them and transplanted them and gifted them. This year ours had seventeen blooms.

Oh, there's more, plenty more. Once she dug a mountain hemlock and a larch from the edge of a backcountry fire ring with flat palm-sized rock and carried them out twenty miles in her backpack between dirty socks and

Nalgene. She's eased dogwood seedlings from irrigation ditches. Another book on our shelf, *Propagation of Pacific Northwest Native Plants* by Rose, Chachulski, and Haase, has no nickname, but our dog-eared copy does have this passage bracketed in ballpoint: "When transplanting, place Pacific dogwood in a ring of native shrubs to protect the lower trunk and branches from sunburn." She did, and we now have a row of dogwoods on the path to our house, some taller than me. We also have three glorious tiger lilies right by our frost-free spigot, tiger lilies with shy nodding sepals curved backwards, orange with black spots. (Why not stripes?) The *Pojar* claims that Coast Salish people dried the bulbs and cooked them in soups with meat or fish.

Why does she do it? When we built our cabin in the woods a decade ago we tore out a swath of forest. Maybe this is penance? I doubt it. We've also changed the climate of the earth, the two of us and the rest of our ever-growing clan, so maybe she'd claim that this is "assisted migration," a way to salvage species that are displaced by climate change. Nah. She doesn't move them far enough, a few miles perhaps, from public land to private, from one drainage to the next, walking distance always from our cabin, even if it's a long walk. There's no guilt involved, no high-minded-ness—the rescue argument, even, doesn't hold much water since seeds disperse even when stalks are chopped—not even any symbiosis. The seeds don't need us, and we don't need them. We could buy native plants or, hell, hollyhocks. But there is something in the genes, I think, something she shares with the Coast Salish and the Quileute. What is it? I wonder. Something hard-wired for survival, some deep connection to the earth?

I watch her stooped over a section of browned up lupine between rock talus and a blue lake, cupping a handful of lupines-to-be, funneling them into the baggie. At home, she'll plant them and fence them and water them and coddle them, and she'll keep a mental map of where each has come from. For now, she turns and throws her daypack over her shoulder and grins.

"Let's go," she says.

It's glee. ❁

> ## Out of town guests, coerced into an innocent hike with her, are likely to be corrupted straight away.

Organicize Me

By Michael A. Stusser

Collage by Rachael Davis

Editor's Note:
*Michael Stusser's "Organicize Me" was originally pub-
lished in February 2007 in* Seattle Weekly. *We updated the
statistics (noted at the end of the article) in 2011. —Z.K.*

I've made more failed New Year's resolutions than
Charlie Sheen and Courtney Love combined. Lose a dozen
pounds, quit smoking, slow down, speed up, get organized,
drink less, exercise more—all abandoned within hours of
the drunken promise. But this year, my editors at Seattle
Weekly came to me with an offer I couldn't refuse: Go the
opposite of Super Size Me and eat only organic food 24/7
for the month of January—and be paid handsomely for it.
No Doritos, Big Macs, Star-
burnt coffee, brewskies, Red
Bull, or Frankenfoods of any
kind. And, if by going organic,
I help save the planet, all the
better.

Clearly, the first stop on
this assignment would have to
be the notorious PCC.

Since 1953, Puget Consum-
ers Co-op Natural Markets
have served as the state's
Birkenstock capital; and, with
40,000 members, it's the largest natural food co-op in the
nation. Once inside, there's
more information alongside
items than you'll get in *Mother Jones*, a bulk food section
that looks like a grain refinery, teaching labs that clearly
involve mung beans and re-education, and even an in-store
nutritionist.

Perusing the deli case at the West Seattle branch, I
begin to fathom the difficulty of my journey: Though soy
burgers ($3.99), teriyaki drumettes ($8.99), and Brus-
sels sprouts look nominally appetizing, the majority of
the items contain nonorganic ingredients, and thus don't
meet my newfound standards. (To qualify for the USDA
Organic seal, at least 95 percent of the ingredients must be
organic.)

"If you don't cook—even something simple—you're in
trouble," warns PCC's director of public affairs, Trudy Bialic. Looks like trouble. "Prepared foods are going to have
too many ingredients to keep track of and are also more
costly. You're also going to want to eat in season."

I have no idea what she's talking about. Adjusting for
her audience, Bialic tries another tack: "Listen, transi-
tional foods are important for people making big changes.
You want to enjoy your food, and it's OK to have a can

of Amy's lentil soup once in a while, or a frozen organic
pizza, or even some popcorn. It's a slow process: None of
us can change overnight."

Really? Where were you two days ago when I decided
to change—overnight?

Within 72 hours, I've become aware of changes in my
body. These results, of course, aren't scientific: The sight
of blood—especially my own—makes me faint; and without health insurance, I can hardly afford to piss in a cup,
much less order lab tests. Still, I feel cleaner somehow, less
toxic.

While my mind is sharp, my energy level is more slug-
gish than normal—perhaps due to the loss of artificial col-
ors and preservatives in my diet, which are linked to hyper-
activity (in schoolchildren,
anyway). Luckily, I've got
the organic antidote: regular
doses of caffeine. Purely by
accident, I've been drinking
organic coffee for years at
my favorite espresso shops,
Java Bean and Caffe Ladro.
I may starve to death this
month, but at least I'll be
jacked up.

One other medical note:
My appetite has increased.
Specifically, I'm hungry for
a Dick's burger.

After a decade of debate
over what would constitute "organic" food, the U.S. Department of Agriculture laid down its national standards for
certification in 2002. (It should be noted that the first set
of guidelines was heavily influenced by agribusiness and
was significantly more toxic than current standards, until
over 325,000 citizens raised hell and had the regulations
toughened up.)

For organic food to wear the USDA Organic badge of
honor, it must be produced without conventional pesticides, sewage sludge, genetic engineering, fertilizers made
from synthetic ingredients, or ionizing radiation. "Natural"
foods, on the other hand, while without artificial flavoring
or chemical preservatives, may contain ingredients that
were grown with pesticides or genetically modified.

Organic meat, eggs, poultry, and other milk products
can't contain antibiotics or growth hormones. Regulations
also deal with the introduction of new animals to the herd
and even the handling of manure, ensuring runoff doesn't
pollute waterways.

In addition to eliminating nasty toxins from the food
chain, certified organic farmers are also required to empha-
size renewable resources on the homestead, minimize ero-

> Within 72 hours, I've become aware of changes in my body. These results, of course, aren't scientific: The sight of blood—especially my own—makes me faint; and without health insurance, I can hardly afford to piss in a cup, much less order lab tests. Still, I feel cleaner somehow, less toxic.

sion, and conserve soil and water in their processes. Even the packaging is scrutinized, making it doubtful those eggs will be encased in bubble wrap anytime soon.

Yet certified organic is clearly not a politically correct cure-all. Though the organic industry prides itself on a kinder, gentler process in regard to the environment, the entire system is still not fully regulated. While César Chávez and company may have successfully banned the

> **Still, wouldn't it be easier to spray the fields with chemicals? "Oh, definitely," Stout adds. "Herbicides and pesticides are like an insurance program for conventional folks. Thing is, if you abuse the land, you'll eventually run out of property. It's Manifest Destiny; it's why people kept having to move West."**

short-handled hoe in the 1970s, for example, the organic label doesn't assure consumers that laborers receive health benefits for harvest-related injuries or have rights to organize. In fact, organic farm owners formed the most vocal opposition to a ban on hand weeding—the backbreaking alternative to applying pesticides—presented to the California Occupational Safety and Health Administration in 2004. Hence, a "sweat-free food" campaign is currently making the rounds among grassroots activists and the Organic Consumers Association, adding yet another potential label to your USDA Organic, homegrown, Certified Humane, Fair Trade, sustainable cherries.

Some organic growers are less than thrilled with the current USDA standards and have created their own seals of approval. Hard-core cultivators use terms like "biodynamic farming," which prepares homeopathic recipes to enrich the soil, and *terroir*—French for "the essence of the place" —which tosses a spiritual and cosmic element into the mix. And pioneers such as Eden Foods won't use the USDA seal even though they're certified, believing that their practices of small-scale, sustainable, cooperative farming go "beyond organic."

David Lively of the Organically Grown Company, a Eugene, Oregon-based wholesaler, isn't so keen on the

term. "[The] problem with 'beyond organic' is that it gives away the organic part, which was a hard-fought battle. I like 'organic and beyond,' because we can do even more. The current standards allow us to talk to the feds about the Farm Bill and try to increase research dollars. It doesn't go far enough in terms of sustainability and labor, but it's a great start."

PCC's Bialic puts the organic labeling in perspective. "Let's let the baby grow up a little before we throw him out," she says. "The organic standards are only four years old; they're evolving. They may not be perfect, but they're the best thing we've had happen in food since bologna and Wonder Bread."

Nationwide, organic food is booming. Last year, over two-thirds of Americans purchased an organic product. According to the Organic Trade Association, organics accounted for 2.5 percent of all food and beverage sales nationwide, with 2006 sales increasing to over $15 billion (from less than $4 billion a decade earlier). While the organic market has soared over 15 percent per year since 1990, nonorganic food companies have gained less than 5 percent over the same time period.

"The problem now is really supply versus demand," notes Barbara Haumann of the Organic Trade Association. With demand increasing, organic farmers (usually with 100 acres or less) have had a hard time keeping up, leading to periodic dairy shortages and producers unable to feed larger stores such as Costco and QFC. "In a recent study of organic food producers," Haumann adds, "52 percent said that the lack of organic raw materials is limiting what can be made. There's just not enough organic acreage right now."

While more than a million acres of certified organic farmland were added over the last four years, bringing the total to 2.5 million acres, that's chump change when compared to total farmland. Organic is still less than one-half of 1 percent of all cropland. One reason may be that small farms are dropping like flies. In the last decade, over 650,000 family farms have bit the dust.

But here in Washington state, organic agriculture has boomed bigger than ugly condos in Belltown. According to Miles McEnvoy, organic program director at the Washington Department of Agriculture, the organic industry has grown over a hundredfold since 1988. Today, there are 1,000 certified organic operators in the state, 630 farms, and organic sales of $438 million.

Andrew Stout's Full Circle Farm sits on 260 acres in Carnation. Though he can't use a crop duster, he sees huge advantages to being organic. "We farm about 75 differrnt fruits, vegetables, and herbs," says Stout. "With all the [crop] rotation we do, we aren't putting all our eggs in one basket."

Still, wouldn't it be easier to spray the fields with chemicals? "Oh, definitely," Stout adds. "Herbicides and pesticides are like an insurance program for conventional folks. Thing is, if you abuse the land, you'll eventually run out of property. It's Manifest Destiny; it's why people kept having to move West."

Going organic is not as easy as putting a bug sprayer away in the barn, though. The transition from conventional fields to organic takes a minimum of three years, allowing soil to be free from pesticides and synthetic fertilizers and farmers time to learn the trade. Worms eventually come back, too.

Jay Gordon's family has been dairy farming in the Chehalis Valley for 134 years. He brought home his first organic herd on September 1, 2006. The hardest part of Gordon's transition wasn't eliminating the chemicals from his soil, or filling out the copious paperwork for USDA certification, but that he missed seeing his original group of heifers every day.

Just call me Organic Superman: While my entire family has been down for the count with some disgusting phlegmy cough, I am healthy as an ox.

"Luckily, my older cows are just across the river," he says. "So I get to go visit them at my neighbors'."

According to Gordon, who is also executive director of the Washington State Dairy Federation, Seattle has the highest percentage (11 percent) of citizens who purchase organic dairy products in the country. But there's still room for growth: Two years ago, Washington state had three organic dairies; today there are 52. By the end of 2007, 5 percent of all dairy farms will be organic. (Realizing that planting crunchy granola crops is the fastest-growing field in agriculture, Washington State University has created the nation's first organic farming degree program.)

Gordon says part of the reason for this growth is the terrain: "We've used chicken and cow manure since the early '80s and always grazed our cows. But it's just easier to do here than in Kansas or South Dakota. It just fits my farm. If we had to milk 1,000 cows, you'd have to haul in organic feed from somewhere and it may not work."

Gordon has something else he wants to say about my (albeit temporary) all-organic diet: "I know you have to pay a little more for organic milk, and farmers get a little of that back, and we appreciate it. So thank you for switching over."

"Is this all organic?" I ask my lovely wife, as we sit over a fine-looking meal of pasta puttanesca. "Pretty much," she replies. "The pasta's organic whole wheat from Trader Joe's, the olive oil is definitely organic, along with the basil and olives. But I'm not sure about the red-pepper flakes. I know it's all natural, but I'm not so sure it's organic."

Not *sure*? We're not *sure* if we have sewage sludge or traces of mercury in our meal? Not *sure* if the children are ingesting endosulfan, a relative of DDT? Not *sure* if our nervous systems are being compromised? Not *sure*? "Well, *be* sure from now on," I say, pushing my plate to the side and focusing on the organic salad before me. "You know," I add, "67 million birds are killed each year from pesticides that are sprayed on the fields. I hope you're OK with that."

If looks could kill.

Visiting other people's houses is going to be a problem, too. I've always hated nebbishes with "food issues": lactose-intolerant, vegan, alcoholic, shellfish-sensitive, peanut-allergic pains in the ass. "Is there cheese in that? I can't do dairy; it gives me gas." Now I'd be one of them. "Uh, Cheri, I know you slaved for hours over this fantastic jambalaya, but I'm gonna need to see the receipts for all the ingredients. I'm on a bit of a health binge, and I don't think you care as much about what goes into your body as I do. It's not you, Cheri. It's me. Go ahead and enjoy your pesticide-laden feast. I'll just sit over here with my chickpea yogurt."

Just call me Organic Superman: While my entire family has been down for the count with some disgusting phlegmy cough, I am healthy as an ox. Could this be a result of organic produce having more antioxidants than conventional fruits and veggies? (This has to do with the plant's own defense system having to fight off critters, rather than letting pesticides take care of it.) In addition, thanks to pre-ripened picking, longer storage, and more processing, conventional crops typically have far fewer nutrients. So long as there's no organic kryptonite, it looks like I'm good to go!

Yet quandaries abound. Like a deer in the headlights, I'm frozen in the fresh produce section of Whole Foods (aka Whole Paycheck), with too many choices. In one hand, an organic apple from Brewster, Washington; in the other, an organic orange from California.

"Buying close to home is always cool," enthuses David Lively. "Local is happenstance. Organic requires motivation. If you can get it both ways, do it."

If I were a "locavore" (i.e., health food nuts living on fare grown in "foodsheds" within 100 miles of where they live), this would be a no-brainer. "The issue is, really, 'What do you know about the food you're eating?'" explains Goldie Caughlan, PCC's nutrition education manager. "Support the organic label, *and* know who grows it."

But shouldn't I always buy from local farmers? "For the first 10 years of my life, we only ate what we grew or hunted," replies Caughlan. "But sometimes you're in the mood for some citrus."

Finding organic lunch options has also proven to be problematic. Ninety-five percent of my midday meals prior to the new year involved teriyaki or Taco Time. Now it's "make your own at home," which is difficult enough without having to read every damn label.

To compound matters, whereas my bologna that has a first name (it's O-S-C-A-R) can last in the fridge for several months without turning green or smelling of old tennis shoes, the organic sandwich meat I bought last week has turned rancid—the cost of not being filled with nitrates and preservatives. This part of the organic experiment does not please me or my wallet.

As the weeks wear on, I find myself shoving anything with the word "organic" stamped on it into my mouth. The most convenient choices, unfortunately, are all sweets: Morning Peanut Butter Bars ($3 from the Flying Apron Organic Bakery), Fabe's Mini-Macaroons ($4.89), Nature's Path Vanilla Animal Cookies ($3.29), Country Choice Double-Fudge Brownies ($3.69), and Coconut Curry Bars from 3400 Phinney ($3.29). A guy can get plenty fat on an unbalanced organic diet, and I've got the new belly to prove it (at this point, I've put on 5 pounds). I wonder if an organic fat cell looks any different during liposuction from a nonorganic fat cell?

"We're not talking about an organic apple that can cure cancer. Instead, it's about trying to maximize chances that you're healthy and will remain healthy," says Dr. Charles Benbrook, chief scientist of the Organic Center. "Americans have the most diverse diet in the world, with the most choices, but two-thirds of our population is dying from food-related diseases or health problems. There was a report by the USDA last year that said it all: We're overfed and undernourished. People like you, seeking out organic, will get unexpected benefits: a nutrient-dense diet—more bang for their calories."

Still, even Mormons need a vice to get by: cigars, string

To be honest, when the New Roots tub arrives at my house, I have absolutely no idea what to do with a majority of the goods: Parsnips? Gold beets? Yukon potatoes? Celery root?

cheese, porn—something. Luckily, I discovered an organic vodka called Square One. The production's as simple as a moonshine-makin' home distillery: Take pure spring water from the Snake River, add organic North Dakota rye, and distill using natural fermentation techniques. Shake and pour. (Result: hammered. Verrry nice!) Plus, the bottle's groovy, and can be reused as a vase.

In the U.S., regular produce travels an average of 1,500 miles between the farm and your grocery store. Food miles, they're called. The farther products travel, the more energy and gas are used to get the stuff to you. Buying local can cut a thousand miles off, but I still had to constantly schlepp to PCC for organic chow, eating up valuable time and precious gas in my Volvo. That's where companies like New Roots Organics come in.

"Basically, I'm doing organic shopping for 400 people," explains owner Carolyn Boyle. For $35 every other week, New Roots delivers a bin of 12-15 organic fruits and vegetables to your door. "The majority of my clients are super busy but want to eat well and don't always know what to buy," adds Boyle. "Our service gives them a big variety and makes sure there's always quality fruit around."

To be honest, when the New Roots tub arrives at my house, I have absolutely no idea what to do with a majority of the goods: Parsnips? Gold beets? Yukon potatoes? Celery root? For the cuisine-challenged among us, Boyle tosses suggested recipes into each bin. This week: kale, squash, and pancetta pie; risotto with spinach and herbs; and blue cheese with those odd-looking beets.

There are pros and cons to having the O-Bin delivered. Pro: Fruits and vegetables are good for you; the more they're around, the more chance you'll shove an Anjou pear slice into your face instead of a Cheeto. Con: Who the hell can eat a giant container of baby turnips, cauliflower, and countless apples every other week? In our case, leftovers are going to our guinea pig, and gee, his coat looks terrific!

Generally speaking, buying organic no longer means getting your produce from a grassroots co-op in Duvall. Mirroring conventional agribusiness, half of all organic sales come from the largest 2 percent of farms. And even though organic represents only 2.5 percent of all food and drink purchases, the U.S. organic industry will do over $16 billion this year in consumer sales, and everyone—even Wal-Mart—is grabbing a piece of the action.

Today, 13 of the top 20 multinational food manufacturers own an organic brand. General Mills bought Cascadian Farm, Hershey's snatched up Dagoba chocolate, Dean Foods purchased milk-maker Horizon, Coca-Cola took over Odwalla, and even M&M Mars owns Seeds of Change. (For a great chart illustrating how the big fish are buying the little organic ones, go to www.msu.edu/~howardp.)

"It's possible to gain something from the conventional guys," notes David Lively. "If they bring their labs and expertise in nutrition or quality control, that's a good thing. But if they say, 'OK, hippie, get out of the way,' sit's a problem. It's important these megacorporations don't knock out the visionaries in the company. They need to do more than just follow the law; they need to move the agenda forward. It's still buyer beware. Consumers can't let up just because there's a seal."

With huge volumes come lower standards, factory farms, and suppliers from anyone but your local grower. According to the Organic Consumer Association, Wal-Mart is currently filling its shelves with organic foods and ingredients from as far away as China and Brazil. Though all imported organic products must still be certified, questions about being able to grow anything "healthy" in areas with horrific air quality and acid rain remain. (Wal-Mart may be jumping too fast into the fray, as it is being sued by the Cornucopia Institute for passing nonorganic food off as organic.)

Lively, who sells to natural markets along the I-5 corridor, is plenty concerned about corporate farms and Wal-Mart's treatment of growers, but claims it's all relative. Says Lively: "I had just finished some speech at a convention that bashed Wal-Mart's practices when this lady came up and said, "You know, it's easy for you to pop off and play elitist in the West. It's the natural food mecca. If you live in Kansas City, like I do, you go to Wal-Mart for organic food. It's all you've got.'"

For plenty of families, buying organic produce is less of a priority than simply putting fresh food on the table. For those who must pick and choose, the Environmental Working Group (EWG) has established a "dirty dozen": produce that, due to high pesticide residue, absolutely should be purchased organic. Apples and nectarines top the list, followed by cherries, peaches, pears, raspberries, imported grapes, strawberries, bell peppers, celery, potatoes, and spinach. If you can't go 100 percent organic, certain fruits and vegetables—due to how they're grown and ease of cleaning—are less likely to be contaminated, including bananas, mangos, pineapples, corn, onions, avocados, peas, and cauliflower.

And don't think you can just peel a nonorganic apple and be done with it. "You may eliminate a majority of any chemicals," explains Dr. Benbrook. "But you'll also get rid of 60 percent of the nutrients that are in the skin and the layer just under it."

For plenty of families, buying organic produce is less of a priority than simply putting fresh food on the table. For those who must pick and choose, the Environmental Working Group (EWG) has established a "dirty dozen": produce that, due to high pesticide residue, absolutely should be purchased organic. Apples and nectarines top the list, followed by cherries, peaches, pears, raspberries, imported grapes, strawberries, bell peppers, celery, potatoes, and spinach.

"This kale is so tasty!" exclaims Seattle Tilth director Karen Luetjen, pointing at a barren, winterized section of Tilth's Demonstration Garden in Wallingford. "If you'd like, you can make a little to-go salad right now, add some broccoli florets over there, that lettuce, and you're on your way."

The dirt diggers at Seattle Tilth have been promoting organic gardening since 1978. Today, Seattle Tilth runs over 300 programs that reach 15,000 citizens a year, including City Chickens 101 and a kids' class, *Don't Crush That Bug!*

Living off the land, of course, is not the newest concept around. Seattle already has over 1,900 organic P-Patch plots, and while there may not be much sun, most of the patches are gardened year-round. If you want in, though, stand in line: There's a wait list for almost every patch in town.

Yao Fou Hin Chao works with over 600 members of the Iu Mien community in various P-Patches along Rainier Avenue and MLK Way, which are the primary sources of food for many Laotian, Vietnamese, and Chinese immigrants. Says Yao: "Many come to me, say, 'I need food. I know how to garden, but I need plot.' My job is to teach them how to garden in this area. Laos climate is easy, like California. Here is different—all new crops, new time to plant, new method."

Yao also teaches his gardeners to grow mustard greens, beets, and bottle gourds, plus corn, tomatoes, and cucumbers that can be frozen and eaten all winter. "Some garden for therapy, for experiment, for fun, to meet others," explains Yao. "For me, to help my people eat, and eat healthy."

So does Yao ever *buy* organic food? "I don't eat organic from store. I know where it is, but can't afford. When I see PCC, I walk by window and don't feel bad. I have my own produce."

Mark Musick has been involved in the Tilth movement since 1974 and has worked with organizations ranging from farmers markets to the Vashon CoHousing Community. "Food is a way to reconnect with the culture," Musick begins. "After all, the word *culture* comes from *cultivate*. Food is our most intimate link to the earth. It just makes sense that you'd want to know where your food comes from. And that's a great place to start."

One way people connect, he suggests, is by meeting growers at farmers' markets, where more than half the vendors nationally are organic. In the greater Seattle area, farmers' markets have expanded from 12 in 1996 to 86 in 2006. On any given weekend during the summer, 67,000 people will shop at a farmers' market.

Another direct connection is through CSAs (Community Supported Agriculture), where small farms market directly to consumers through regular drop-off locations around the state. There are 50 CSA farms in Western Washington, serving 4,000 families. At Carnation's Full Circle Farm, over 75 percent of the company's business comes from 2,500 CSA customers, including schools, Starbucks, Fred Hutchinson, Amgen, and various community centers.

Full Circle's Stout understands that what we really want is the ideal of the farm pastoral based on Old MacDonald:

the red barn, the oak tree with a tire swing. "In recent surveys, the No. 1 thing customers say is important is where the food is grown," says Stout. "A sense of place: people you can trust. After that come quality, the price, and if it's organic."

Are you cool that Kashi is really Kellogg's, or would you prefer getting your granola from Gary in Gold Bar? And if your corn is husked by some kid in Bangkok for 4 cents an hour, then shipped over on a nuclear submarine, is organic really the most important part of your purchase?

In the end, Musick explains, the issues of organic vs. nonorganic aren't the most important. "The key is making local connections to the earth," he says. "If you ask PCC where their black beans come from, or a lot of their bulk items, they'll tell you it comes from China. What we need is Community Supported Agriculture. We're building a better constituency for a better type of agriculture, and now you've been enrolled."

I am exhibiting signs of the dreaded E. coli. And believe me, I know what the hell they are: In 1993, my pal Mike Schiller and I ate undercooked burgers at a fast-food restaurant and got the runs, massive stomach cramps, and nasty gas for weeks on end. Not to mention blood in the stool. (Sorry if you are eating while reading this.)

Good news: Turns out my E. coli scare was just too much dried organic fruit in one sitting. Doc says I basically ate the equivalent of 13 plums, six apples, and 11 apricots the other day. Oh, and the blood? Dried cherries.

With five days remaining in my monthlong experiment, I'm feeling vigorous and in a helluva lot better shape than that guy in *Super Size Me* was at this point. My pulse (64) and blood pressure (116/80) are slightly lower than before, I'm sleeping like a log (as usual), and like our guinea pig, my hair has a new, beautiful luster.

Fighting off my Mighty-O Donut addiction, I've finally figured out *how* to eat organic (a little endive salad here, a trip to the all-organic Sterling Cafe there), and my weight is back to normal. The constant produce from New Roots Organics has changed the color of my urine from the bright lemon-lime of Gatorade to a more foamy consistency and the color of a tangerine, indicating more beets, rhubarb, and vitamin C in my diet.

When I started talking to natural food junkies at the beginning of the month, they would rave about particular organic fruits or vegetables I *had* to try, as if I'd recently been dropped here from the barren Planet Zoron. David Lively was obsessed with a California orange that only came around once a year; Tilth's Karen Luetjen carried on about homegrown tomatoes at their annual tastings; and PCC's Goldie Caughlan had a food-gasm over Nash Hubor's carrots from Dungeness Valley. Thing is, it's true: At times, organic tastes better. Way better. And isn't flavor a huge part of the eating experience?

The final tally had me losing 3 pounds and more cash than I was comfortable with. My family of four's food budget is usually around $800 per month; this month, thanks to several $6.99 pints of raspberries, $13 wedges of cheese, $21 steaks, and $7 grapefruits, our grand total was $1,372.51—a 58 percent increase.

All in all, organic food isn't always affordable, or even healthy. (Try living off Tostitos Organic Tortilla Chips and Natural American Spirit cigarettes.) And the more you think about the social issues surrounding the food on your plate, the more complicated things get. How many miles per gallon does the tractor on the organic farm get? Do you need apples from New Zealand, or is there a local alternative? What's the relationship between farmhand wages and farm owner profits? Are you cool that Kashi is really Kellogg's, or would you prefer getting your granola from Gary in Gold Bar? And if your corn is husked by some kid in Bangkok for 4 cents an hour, then shipped over on a nuclear submarine, is organic really the most important part of your purchase?

I had wanted my choices to be black and white: Organic equals good, everything else equals bad. But now the gray is all around me. The growers aren't necessarily families, friendly, or in the business for politically correct reasons. The products aren't always local, regional, or even national. The whole thing made me angry, confused, and jonesing for a Twix bar.

Still, some organizations are trying to address issues beyond land stewardship and ecology, paying attention to socially just food systems: the communal utopia that counterculture types established in the 1960s. These hippie homesteaders understood that eating right is as simple as knowing where your food comes from, and if that's an organic garden in your backyard, more power to you.

Next month, I've actually decided to kick my diet up a notch for an entirely different reason. Turns out, cooking food—organic or not—destroys much of its protein, vitamins, and minerals, making your immune system work overtime, aging you faster, and increasing the chance of deadly disease. Well, no thanks! I'm now eating truly old-school: 100 percent raw. Bring on the fresh seaweed, egg yolks, and celery juice. It's go time. ❀

Afterward

Since 2007, the organic market has continued to grow. According to the Organic Trade Association, organic food accounted for 3.7% of nationwide food and beverage sales in 2009, an 1.2% increase from 2005.

According to USDA data, U.S. producers dedicated approximately 4.8 million acres of farmland (cropland and pasture) to organics in 2008. This is almost double the 2.5 million acres mentioned in Strusser's article. Between 2002 and 2008, there has been an average 15% annual increase in cropland acreage across the U.S., however, the overall adoption level is still low; organics only accounted for 0.7% of all cropland in 2008, from 0.5% in Strusser's article. Organic vegetables are doing well: fresh produce the top-selling category in organic retail sales. Livestock was also beginning to catch up in 2008, but not as much as predicted (5%). In 2008, 2.7% of dairy cows and 1.5% of layer hens were managed under certified organic systems. The top U.S. crops (corn, soybeans and wheat) are almost all grown non-organically. Organic corn only accounts for 0.2% of the total corn sold here in the U.S., organically grown soybeans account for 0.2% of the total, and wheat only 0.7% of the total amount sold.—Z. K.

THEY MAY NOT HAVE A PULSE, BUT, BOY, CAN THESE GUYS TALK!

EVER WANTED TO ASK . . .

Napoleon about his complex or van Gogh about the whole ear episode? Thomas Jefferson about his hypocritical slavery stance or if Frida might consider a brow wax? *Here's your chance!*

Now, in *The Dead Guy Interviews*, modern-day journalist Michael Stusser chats with forty-five of the most famous personalities of all time, asking them probing and illuminating questions about their lives, conquests, and what's on their iPods.

THE DEAD GUY INTERVIEWS PARTICIPANTS INCLUDE:

Alexander the Great
Beethoven
Buddha
Julius Caesar
Caligula
Catherine the Great
Cleopatra

Confucius
Crazy Horse
Salvador Dali
Albert Einstein
Benjamin Franklin
Sigmund Freud
Genghis Khan

Henry VIII
Joan of Arc
Robert Johnson
Leonardo da Vinci
Mao Zedong
Karl Marx
Montezuma

Mozart
Nostradamus
Edgar Allan Poe
William Shakespeare
Sun Tzu
Mae West
Oscar Wilde

MICHAEL A. STUSSER

www.michaelstusser.com

PENGUIN BOOKS
A member of Penguin Group (USA) www.penguin.com

Mango Collage by Mae Fayne

How to Eat a Mango

by Carolyne Wright

"In the Garden of Eden, the fruit
of the Tree of Knowledge of Good and Evil
was most likely a pomegranate or a mango."
        —National Public Radio

First, you need patience, a straight-
bladed parer, and fingers keen to grip
the skin's deep green and rosey-pink
blush. Ringless fingers nimble enough

to slip the stainless blade
like a blessing into peach-firm
flesh, and resist the temptation

of cuticle cuts and thumb stubs. Or
a man would do the trick, a man warm
as pomegranate sap in spring: new
Adam who won't wait for fruitfall

or your woman's swell against his hands—
the weight of mistranslated apple
in his palm. A man who'll hand-

over-foot-it up the scaled trunk
to where the ready clusters nestle
among glossy night-crowned leaves
and with an artist's deft wrist

twist one mammary-heavy mango
from its stem-socket, wrestle his burden
down from the tree, his taste buds'

first succulence. A man who'll open
his mouth to take the ripe flesh on
his tongue, and forgive his woman
their mutual myth-ridden sin.

A man who's not afraid to share
his skin, or mingle his juices
and go with your flow, your

glow, who'll fill your mouth
like Persephone's with pomegranate
seeds, and wash down the mango's tart
sweet meat with Green Mamba

cordial—its logo a leaf-colored serpent
wound 'round the bottle,
electric eyes a-glitter.

The Blossoming Fiction of Carleen Brice

by Sandra Knauf

I closed my eyes and inhaled. The mint smelled like a just-sliced orange, but not as strong. It was a more relaxing kind of scent. I put a leaf in my mouth. The taste was a mixture of orange peel and grass . . . When I opened my eyes, she was grinning at me, happy to see somebody else could appreciate her problem child.

—from *Orange Mint and Honey*

olorado author Carleen Brice's first novel, *Orange Mint and Honey* (Ballantine Books), has been a continuing sensation since it first appeared in 2008. It won a Break-out Author of the Year Award, African American Literary Awards, and a 2009 First Novelist Award, Black Caucus of the American Library Association. In 2010 it was made into a Lifetime TV movie "Sins of the Mother," and this March it won the Outstanding TV Movie award at the NAACP Image Awards. Brice's second book, *Children of the Waters* is also enjoying critical acclaim and she is currently at work on her third book, *Calling Every Good Wish Home*.

I met Brice at AuthorFest 2010 in Manitou Springs, Colorado where she was a keynote speaker. As garden-ers do, we bonded over our shared enthusiasm for grow-ing plants, and I was thrilled when she agreed to do an interview for *Greenwoman Magazine*'s first issue.

What struck me, after reading both of Brice's books, which focus on women and their often problematic and complex but intensely loving familial relationships, is the role the garden plays in her narratives—as a meta-phor with subtle but unmistakable power, and as a recur-rent scene of healing ritual.

One parched, blustery January day we connected to have a chat about creating both gardens and fiction.

Greenwoman: **I've seen pictures of your front garden and I love it! It's very xeric yet has almost a "West-ern cottage garden look," with lots of hardy, color-ful, drought-tolerant flowers, big pink sandstone boulders—and those beautiful roses! What was your process? Were you inspired by Lauren Ogden? [Og-den is Colorado's most famous garden designer—she promotes lush yet drought-tolerant gardens that bring the larger Colorado landscape into play.]**

Brice: [Laughs]: I have heard of her but haven't read any of her books. The front was all grass when we moved in and it stayed that way for a few years. We thought it was crazy to water a ginormous lawn with southern exposure, so we xeriscaped it with help from my husband's brother, a landscape architect who lives in Seattle. He suggested plants, and we would visit gar-den centers and see if we liked them. We also walked around and looked in other people's gardens, visited the botanic gardens, and researched drought-tolerant plants there. We made lists. That's how we put it together. Then friends gave me plants and plants just showed up, you know [laughs], because that's how it works. Or I'd go into a garden center and fall in love with something that was not in the plan at all but I liked it and put it in the ground, and we'd see how it'd do. So some of it was trial and error.

Greenwoman: **Did your brother-in-law provide a design?**

Brice: He gave us a design, but we didn't stick to it because we're not designers and one of the things I think about is that gardening is different than landscaping. Landscaping is an art; a landscaper is really into efficiency and making it beautiful and using the land well, and all those things a gardener is also interested in, but, for me, a gardener also says, "Oh, that plant is pretty, I'm going to stick it right here and see if it will grow, just because! Or somebody says, "I have all these extra irises that I'm going to throw out," and you say, "You're going to throw them away? I'll take them! I know I don't have a place for them but I'll find a place." The idea of throwing them away just sounds awful.

Greenwoman: **I, too, hate to see useable plants thrown away, and I agree with the gardener-versus-designer insight. We have to honor our individual styles. You and your husband garden together. Are you of the same mind on style?**

Brice: Dirk is way more orderly in life than I am so he would prefer if the area where we put the California poppies be the only area in the yard where we have California poppies. I'm more like, Dude, you're going to try to control California poppies, good luck to you, because I can't see that happening. [Laughs.] For me it's more like we didn't do what you're supposed to do, what most people do with these repeated areas of flowers, we did these sort of fields. He'd say, "Okay, only the poppies in that part," and I'd say, "No." So now we have poppies everywhere and yarrow everywhere and he hates the yarrow and you know, once you've got all this yarrow, you're crazy if you think you're going to stop it.

Greenwoman: **Like mint.**

Brice: Even more so because it seeds everywhere, and I overplanted it, not knowing how much it would spread. I ordered a mix of reds and pinks and whites, and I put in eight plants thinking, these little eight plants will fill this rectangle here, and now it's yarrow everywhere! In May it is one beautiful couple of weeks of yarrow, and then after that it's a pain in the ass. I can understand why he doesn't like it. If I go out there and cut off all the blooms it will rebloom a little bit but it's like cutting a field, and then in the winter it seeds more. Now there are all those seedheads out there, blowing yarrow everywhere, and I don't mind it, but it drives him crazy.

Greenwoman: **Everything's tough and beautiful. Do you grow many herbs? Do you grow vegetables?**

Brice: We have a kitchen garden in the back. There are herbs there that winter over—chives and oregano. It's just wild now, so it's kind of a blanket of wild herbs.

I have done very little vegetable gardening and that's sort of one of the things my husband Dirk and I have gardening disagreements on, because I would put tomatoes and vegetables in the front yard amongst everything and, again, he's into order, so he would not like that.

Greenwoman: **But that's the "in" thing right now. I want to plant some beans out front and have them climb up my fence and the arch over my gate.**

Brice: I know! It makes sense, especially when so often the front yard is no longer lawn anymore. I think, why not? But we'll see, like I said there are a lot of things I put in the garden that we didn't exactly discuss first and some of them he hates, like the yarrow, but one of the things I put in was 'Elijah' blue fescue and that has really spread and he loves it. So I'm thinking, one year I'll do tomatillos and peppers and make a green chili garden.

Greenwoman: **I know you must have orange mint. How did that get into your book?**

Brice: When our garden was coming together, my husband and I would take walks in the neighborhood and pay more attention to other people's yards. At the same time I was writing *Orange Mint and Honey* and that fueled my interest too because my character Nona was a gardener. One day we were walking not too far from where we live and a woman was outside watering. We stopped and admired her garden, and she just gave us the tour. It made an impression on me because she stopped and introduced us to all the plants. [Laughs.] They all had a story—this one was from her daughter, this one from here, very much like in the book. When I asked about the orange mint she told me this story about they make a wonderful tea with it, and she said, "You can have some but it will take over." When we left I told my husband, 'Oh my God, that's going in the book.' And then, of course, it became this whole metaphor for the story.

Greenwoman: **A brilliant metaphor for, among other things, not always being in control, and learning to come to terms with that. The garden plays such a**

strong role in your work. Did you come from a background of gardeners?

Brice: No. It's kind of funny, my mom didn't even have houseplants when I was growing up, but I always liked plants. When I was in college, after my girlfriend and I moved out of the dorm and got an apartment, we both had lots of plants. I remember one year when we were leaving for Christmas break we were trying to figure out how we were going to keep the plants alive while we were gone a month. We put them in the bathtub and put a little water in the tub but the place was so cold that the plants died. It was one of the college student/slumlord things, where you get back and it's 40 degrees and everything's dead. Later I had apartments and as my birthday is at the end of May I would always go to a garden center and get plants and make my pots for the summer. That would be my birthday present to myself, and a kick-off to summer. When I moved into a house it sort of dawned on me, wow, you have all this land—you could try it. And I didn't know what the heck I was doing and for a few years I was trying to garden and it was just a disaster. Then I learned, and my husband got involved, and we got much better at it.

Greenwoman: **Gardening is definitely a live-and-learn experience. Usually learning the hard way. [Laughs.] In** *Children of the Waters*, **Billie, the main character has a koi pond with water lilies, she grows herbs, vegetables, roses. And she also has a "swept yard" in front. I'd like to share a passage from your book. The reader learns that Billie discovered her West African ancestors had "swept yards" in Georgia, where the soil was clay, as it often was in Denver:**

"Nothing appealed more to Billie than picking up a dying tradition of her ancestors. So when they moved in, she dug up the weedy grass and surrounded the dirt with river rocks so the soil wouldn't erode and wind wouldn't blow dirt all over. Most of the neighbors hated it at first. Billie had even overheard a woman driving by comment on "all that ugly-ass dirt." But she swept the dirt every day with a bamboo broom, keeping it tidy and free of weeds, and eventually the clay compacted and was now almost as smooth and glossy as the rocks. These days, people stopped to admire their yard and asked her how she did it. As she answered their questions, she smiled along with the ancestors."

Brice: That came from two places. There are a couple of dirt yards in my neighborhood that are not very beautiful but they are water-wise and people have done it on purpose. They put a few things in pots and have up signs "Use only what you need," to make sure that everybody knows that that's why they're doing it.

As I was doing research for Billie and her interest in the ancestors and such, I learned that in Georgia they do the clay/dirt yards and I just loved that idea, that there would be a link between the southern slave roots and Billie. I knew she would like that.

Greenwoman: **And you paint such a pretty picture!**

Brice: Well, supposedly if you brush it [clay soil], it really can polish and kind of get smooth and pretty. That passage, where it mentions people complaining about her yard until it turns pretty, that came from when we first started our front yard xeriscape. We did it in parts and our neighbors weren't quite sure what the heck we were doing. We took up the grass and ordered recycled wood mulch and we put down a few tons of that and we had these boulders brought in. We did it in the fall so all the way until next spring it was just mulch and rock and one time my husband was outside and he heard a woman stopped at the stop sign in front of our house and she said, "Look at all this ugly-ass rock." About our yard! And we were laughing, like, "It's just the beginning!"

On the garden as a strong metaphor in my books, I really planned that in the first book but in Billie's book, when she's getting closer to being more of a gardener, I didn't want to repeat myself, so I was trying real hard not to make her just like 'Nona junior.' [Nona's the mother in *Orange Mint and Honey*.] I guess it's just such a part of me, it was inevitable that it would bleed into the story.

Greenwoman: **Billie is definitely her own person, but I understand what you're saying. It's the same for any type of art, you can often tell it's the same artist, not only from the style, but from the subject matter. These are the things the artist is most interested in. What is your next book going to be about?**

Brice: Right now I am writing a novel that I'm still trying to get my head around. What I do know is that one of the characters is an interior designer and a home stager for people who are putting their house on the market. I'm thinking some of the same things will come into play, only inside the home, not outside, and I think there's sort of a spiritual aspect to that that will probably come into the story as it has in the other couple of books.

Greenwoman: Ritual is also strong in your novels. I love this passage from *Orange Mint and Honey.* **It's Nona speaking to her daughter, the main character, Shay. Nona's battled alcoholism, and is now trying to earn the trust of her daughter. She says:**

"Some twelve-steppers keep a God box that they put their problems in. but the best way I know to turn over my problems to God is to turn over some dirt.' She dug a shallow hole next to one of the tomato plants. . . 'Write whatever comes to you, whatever you want to let go of,' she said, looking up at me. "Rip up the paper and spread the pieces like mulch. When the paper breaks down, it makes the soil richer. Come spring, your problems will help the plants grow."

Greenwoman: I love it. There were some beautiful rituals in *Children of the Waters, t*oo. **Does ritual play a part in your next book?**

Brice: Yeah, I think so. It's something I'm interested in so it slips in, even when I don't plan it. It's like that quote about how writers don't pick their subject, the subject picks them, and that's really true. I'm sure there are people who have more of a plan, they sit down with a genre, but I think even if you're doing that, even if you say, "I'm going to be a romance writer because romance sells," I think there's also probably something in you that's attracted to that genre, and can understand it and appreciate it in a way that will allow you to write well about it.

Greenwoman: As you write so well in your genre of women's fiction. Thank you so much for agreeing to this interview, Carleen.

Brice: Thank you for inviting me. ❀

new from Ana Maria Spagna

Just released!

Potluck

Community at the Edge of Wilderness

Affectionate, wry, and wise writings that range from Tijuana to Utah's canyon country and, always, back to the remote valley in the North Cascades that Spagna calls home.

"Peels back the reality of living in a small, close community." —David Oates, *City Limits*

ISBN 978-0-87071-591-4 • $18.95 Paperback

Now Go Home

Wilderness, Belonging, and the Crosscut Saw

"Ana Maria Spagna's essays are stubborn, compact, and densely grained as a whitebarked pine at timberline."

—John Daniel, *Winter Creek: One Writer's Natural History*

ISBN 978-0-87071-009-4 • $18.95 Paperback

Oregon State | OSU Press
UNIVERSITY

Available in bookstores or online: http://oregonstate.edu/dept/press

Garden Lessons by Eva Syrovy

I posted the pictures right away. They were adorable, two eleven year olds with beginnings of summer tans, digging, watering, earnestly perusing the backs of seed packets. They were putting in their first garden.

Earlier, my son carried the seeds, his friend the hoe, and I a shovel, as we walked the few blocks to the community garden. The director showed me my plot, and as I spaded and hoed the dirt, I reflected how easy and automatic the task was, even with my sporadic gardening tendencies. History will tell.

Four families that lived in my apartment house in the Czech Republic adopted a whole field once. It must have been a good half acre. We all tilled it one afternoon. We kids tried to get rid of all the weeds, and ended with a manicured few feet; the grownups did the rest, spading up the dirt roughly and ending with something that looked plowed, like a real field. After which the enthusiasm must have died down; nobody was much interested in watering a field that large, and I think we ended up with a few potatoes for our trouble.

This afternoon, as I crumbled the clods in my hands, and sowed my zucchini, lettuce, radish, pea, and bean seeds, I wondered whether the land had been worked before, and by whom. It's a relatively fertile part of the Springs, the floodplain of Fountain and Camp Creek where there had probably been trees even before the European settlers crowded in and created their urban forest. But the history might be even more interesting. We were only a couple of blocks away from the monument marking the Colorado City stockade; had there been a woman in the fort enterprising enough to sow a vegetable garden, or at least a corn field? It would have been fun to find some remains, like the tiny glass bottle I came across in my back yard, which, I like to imagine, held either perfume or opium for some lady of the night over a century ago.

Watering our newly sowed seeds meant opening a tap from a tank. I asked the boys to bring the water to our plot in buckets, but the notion of a limited water supply seemed almost beyond their comprehension. Learning not to splash to cool down, not to spill as they filled and carried buckets, was a brand new challenge.

But when we were finally done, Jake asked if he could have his own garden.

"I want it in the back yard though," he said. "I don't want to take the chance on somebody stealing my vegetables."

Since my yard has no fence, it wouldn't be all that challenging to steal from it, but he seemed convinced of its greater security. I helped them spade up some of the soil, gave them my leftover seeds, and they used what they'd just learned at the community garden.

I remembered, watching them, my own experience—as a thief. After the failure of the communal field, the families in my childhood building did the most logical thing—split it into small plots. And most of the women grew strawberries. Our patch never seemed very verdant, or perhaps we picked it too thoroughly; but the neighboring family's berries were always large, red and luscious. I got into the habit of stopping in their field coming home from school or from playing, picking four or five berries and popping them into my mouth.

One afternoon, as I sat on the steps of the house with the other kids, Mrs. Loubal, the neighbor, came to me with a brimming bowl.

"Here," she said, "you like my berries so much. You can eat all of these right now." I don't remember what I did then. I do remember the most profound feeling of embarrassment of my life. Mrs. Loubal may have acted out of anger, not an instinct to pedagogy. But what she taught me I never forgot.

Gardens are full of lessons. ❀

Illustration by Rachael Davis

Sadie & Ruby ♥ Greenwoman Magazine

Sadie: My mind's still reeling from the thought-provoking articles and stories I read last night.

Ruby: Mine too! *Greenwoman*'s a great mind trip.

Sadie: Can't wait for the next volume. . .

Ruby: Neither can I.

Let's Stay in Touch!

FREE download when you sign up!

We can do just that if you sign up for our weekly newsletter at www.greenwomanmagazine.com.

In return, we'll send you garden writing fabulousness, special offers on our books, and more!

Available through Amazon.com (if that's how you roll).

Or Read Online (the greenest option) for only $2.95 an issue!

Seeds of Sustainability

by Bill McDorman and Stephen Thomas

At the turn of the last century no one owned our seeds. They were part and parcel of the public trust. Nearly every farmer and gardener freely received, saved and shared them. Today, seeds are private property, owned and sold by an elite group of corporate interests. Today, only three companies control 56% of the global seed market.

Because of this, genetic diversity has dwindled at alarming rates. Ninety-six percent of the commercial varieties grown in 1903 are no longer available. Private companies fund most agricultural research, often with the intent to design and patent new organisms for their own gain. Government institutions now make their alliances with the multinational corporations to control the genetic wealth. Alarming stories of "GMOs," "terminator genes," "doomsday seed vaults," and "survival seed banks" regularly make the headlines.

Concern, many would say, is justified. Diversity is the foundation of the strength of any ecosystem. If we irreparably change or destroy the underlying source of our food system—the seeds—our society may very well collapse, and all of our efforts to build a sustainable culture will be for naught. In the view of some observers, our agricultural story is shaping up to be a Greek tragedy, acted out with hubris on a monumental new genetic scale. The President of Novartis Seeds, John Sorenson, exemplified this blind ambition during a 1999 debate with me about GMOs on Idaho Public Television. In response to my concerns over biotechnology's long-term safety, Sorenson proclaimed, "There will be no mistakes. We have the keys to the candy store. We can accomplish quickly what we want now by splicing genes. We can feed the world."

But the truth is, we all know there will be mistakes. This is, in fact, how nature works. The entire history of agriculture can be characterized as humankind taking advantage of the genetic "mistakes" that improved crops. The concern lies in the quality and the consequence of the mistakes being made. In the modern corporate rush to grow large, profitable markets by engineering new life forms, we may have already released enough genetically modified material to sabotage our future food security and public health. We just don't know the outcome yet. While genetic engineering may well play a positive role somewhere in our future, intelligence at this point dictates caution. But there is one thing we can be sure of: genetic engineering in the hands of short-sighted, profit-motivated chemical companies has not been a good idea.

In the face of this brave new world, citizens and farmers alike often react with helplessness, anger and fear.

What can we do?

From the 1970s to Today

I first heard about agriculture's disappearing genetic diversity back in college in the late 1970s. It was then I learned that 96% of the commercial vegetable varieties grown in 1903 were no longer available. After trying to find unique seeds for my own garden and having little luck, I banded together with some fellow gardeners in search of heirlooms. Our quest resulted in founding a seed company of our own—Garden City Seeds—to make these disappearing treasures readily available again. We weren't alone in this vision. The industrialization of agriculture and the centralization of the seed industry had opened a fertile niche for small seed companies targeting a new sustainable agriculture. Except it wasn't actually anything new. The seed world we envisioned at the time closely resembled the world of our grandmothers and grandfathers: a vibrant web of biodiversity and resilience, with every region rich in its own varieties and adapted to its own conditions and culture.

Before long this shared vision blossomed. In 1985 the Missouri Botanical Gardens and the National Garden Association sponsored a national conference for this emerging generation of seed people. A network of visionary, locally minded seed businesses and organizations quickly took root across the country. Operating out of Boise, the pioneering company Seeds Blum gained national exposure selling rare heirlooms. The Iowa-based nonprofit Seed Savers Exchange formed to organize individual gardeners to save their grandparents' seeds. Native Seeds/SEARCH started up in Tucson with the mission to seek out and preserve the seeds from ancient cultures in the Southwest. Many of today's best-known independent seed companies—Johnny's Selected Seeds, Fedco, Territorial, Abundant Life, Garden City Seeds, High Altitude Gardens (another company I founded), and Southern Exposure—companies that focused on finding and marketing seeds adapted to their own regions, rose to prominence during this time.

By the nineties another wave of new seed companies was springing up in reaction to the intensifying industrial storm and disappearing diversity. Largely under the banners of "organic" and "non-GMO," companies like Seeds of Change, High Mowing and Baker Creek entered the seed market with eye-catching new catalogs and high standards of sustainability. By the turn of the 21st century, the Internet helped to bring down the last barriers between seed savers, growers, and potential customers. A renewed era of abundance was underway as countless new seed sources cropped up online. (Several years ago a tomato grower walked into my office after searching the Internet for seeds. He had just discovered roughly 400 seed sources on the web.)

Also by the turn of the century, organic agriculture had become a multi-billion dollar industry, and a number of new companies rose to the challenge to supply seeds for this budding market. Outfits like Seeds of Change, Territorial and Fedco began contracting small organic farmers to grow seed crops, a practice which fueled the beginnings of a nationwide network of organic seed growers. John Navazio and the Organic Seed Alliance set up educational programs to inspire and train these new market farmers and seed growers. A number of operations like Wild Garden Seeds and Siskiyou Seeds grew and marketed their own farm-grown seeds directly to the public. A group known as the Family Farmer Seed Cooperative took this idea one step further, organizing seed growers into regional producers and marketing co-ops. Sound familiar? We are returning full circle to the regionalism, resilience and genetic abundance at the dawn of the last century.

One complicating factor in this return to our agricultural roots is the National Organic Program. Among its many requirements, certified organic growers must buy certified organic seed, if it is available. Although welcomed for its incentives to get the poisons and chemicals out of agriculture, the long-term effect of organic certification on the overall seed picture is a mixed bag. Organic seed is becoming just another industrial market niche. One-size-fits-all, hybrid organic seeds produced by the multinational giants are now beginning to flood the market. At this critical stage, we have lost entirely too much of the world's agricultural genetic diversity. Asking organic farmers to focus on certified organic seed is problematic (and perhaps, catastrophic) since most of the world's remaining diversity is not yet certified. We want—and greatly need—an organic agriculture, but we absolutely need the abundant diversity to sustain it. Until this genetic balance is righted, our focus should be on reintroducing new diversity regardless of whether or not it is government-sanctioned organic. Every farmer can then easily expand diversity under the organic label in one or two seasons by organically growing and saving the seeds from as-yet uncertified crops.

We Hold the Keys to Our Own Candy Store

Once a gardener allows nature to act upon her crops in countless ways, then saves the resulting seeds, she begins to harness the power of nature's elegant built-in genetic feedback system. Even modern plant breeders acknowledge

> Once a gardener allows nature to act upon her crops in countless ways, then saves the resulting seeds, she begins to harness the power of nature's elegant built-in genetic feedback system.

U. S. Seed Saving History

1800:   Thomas Jefferson writes: "The greatest service which can be rendered to any country is to add a useful plant to its culture."

1862:   Famous land-grant universities (such as Michigan, Cornell and Iowa State) are established, in large part to help collect, breed and distribute seeds.

1878:   The USDA allocates at least 1/3 of its budget to collect and freely distribute seeds.

1897-1920s: The Patent and Trade Office supply over 1.1 billion packets of USDA seeds to America's farmers.

1883:   The American Seed Trade Association (ASTA) is formed. It immediately petitions the government to dismantle the USDA seed distribution programs.
Public ownership of seeds becomes threatened.

1924:   After more than 40 years of ASTA lobbying, Congress ends the USDA seed distribution programs. ASTA convinces government that the proper role of publicly funded institutions like land-grant universities is to train plant breeders, perform fundamental research and create raw materials and technologies for private industry to capitalize upon.
Private seed companies seize on this, creating proprietary varieties from the inbred lines and breeding stock developed in public universities.

1930:   The legal origins of the privatization of seeds begins with the Plant Patent Act. This landmark bill allows for plants propagated through cloning to be patented and privately owned, but exempts seed-propagated crops.

1970:   The Plant Variety Protection Act extends intellectual property rights to plants grown from seeds. A wave of seed company mergers and buyouts follow.

1980:   Supreme Court ruling of Diamond vs. Chakrabarty clears the way for the patenting of life forms based on genetic coding. For the first time, the genetic wisdom in a seed can be held as private property. Shortly after this ruling, more than 1,800 such patents are filed.

1992:   Vice President Dan Quayle announces "the coordinated framework" for regulatory reform of biotechnology and GMO crops. This proclamation essentially assures the biotech corporations that no new laws will be passed to regulate their emerging industries. Revealingly, the announcement comes before any genetically modified crops have even been planted—the result of a preemptive, closed-door deal between government and corporate interests.

the advanced ability of nature to create and refine plant varieties. In the *Principles of Plant Breeding*, Robert Allard writes, "In some cases it appears that natural selection may be more discerning than farmers (or plant breeders) in identifying and preserving adaptively superior types, particularly if natural selection is allowed to operate for several to many generations in relevant environments." The seed a gardener produces is already on its way in evolving into a better fit for her growing conditions—site, soil and climate. A gardener can also hand-select the best-tasting, the earliest, the largest of her crops, ensuring those genetic traits are even stronger in the next season.

Some remarkable examples of this process can be found in the colorful tales of farm lore. Take, for instance, the story of James L. Reid, an Ohio farmer who moved to the colder climes of Northern Illinois in 1847. When his favorite yellow dent corn fared poorly in the shorter season, Reid began experimenting. The following year he inter-planted the rest of his dent with locally adapted Indian corn. When the harvest came, Reid saved seed from the ears that resembled his yellow dent. He repeated this process year after year, selecting seed only from those specimens with admirable qualities. Forty years later, Reid's yellow dent corn took the blue ribbon at the Illinois State Fair, and in 1893 it won the gold medal at the World's Fair. His humble corn became the most popular variety of open-pollinated corn grown worldwide during much of the 20th century. All of this success came not from a master breeder or lab geneticist but from one farmer in one field, selecting and saving the best of his seed as an investment into the next growing season.

Or how about the story of Montana gardener Dave Christensen, who struck out on a similar quest for a cold-hardy flour corn thirty years ago? He eventually found more than 70 tough, open-pollinated varieties from Native Americans and homesteaders. None had exactly the qualities he was looking for, so he mixed them up and planted them together. Year after year, Christensen selected, saved, and replanted the best seed. The result? Look no further than Fedco catalog, which praised Christensen's Painted Mountain corn as "the hardiest, fastest-maturing grain corn in the world." Again, this was the work of one farmer, in one field, selecting for specific characteristics. All it takes is reconnecting with the simple process of saving seed.

There's no reason for modern gardeners not to incorporate seed saving into their activities. To put it in economic terms, it is too lucrative an investment to pass up. When a gardener saves her own seeds from plants that flourish

in her particular garden, she carries the best results of one growing season into the next. She invests in her own unique interface with the environment. The investment is not merely compounded—it is exponential. And as an added bonus, it enhances the overall genetic diversity and durability of our agricultural system.

Seed Saving 101

Seed saving does not have to be complicated or overwhelming. Start small. Keep it simple and have fun. Some vegetables and grains are easier to save seed from than others.

Peas, beans, tomatoes and lettuce all have self-pollinating flowers and produce seeds in the first season. They go on the beginners list.

Once successful at saving seeds from the beginners, a gardener can venture into the intermediates: corn, cucumber, muskmelon, radish, spinach, squash and pumpkin. These vegetables are wind- and insect-pollinated and can be contaminated with pollen from unwanted sources. They will also produce seeds the same year as planted. The breeding system of each plant needs to be understood and the appropriate separation distance employed.

The expert vegetables include: beets, Swiss chard, broccoli, cauliflower, cabbage, kale, carrot, escarole, onion, radicchio, chicory, turnip and Chinese cabbage. They all require isolation and produce seeds in the second season after planting.

Isolation distances and other tricks for concurrently growing more than one variety in the same field can be found in most seed saving books (including my own, *Basic Seed Saving*). Carol Deppe's *Breed Your Own Backyard Garden Vegetables* also has an excellent section on selection characteristics and techniques. The tools are in your hands, and the best part is, you are in control. You get to manipulate pollination and keep the seeds for the characteristics you desire. And as Carol reminds us, even if you make mistakes, you get to eat them.

A Return to Reason

We are relearning the powerful potential of saving our own seeds. Just as the resilient and adaptive plants we tend, we are doing what we have always done best: turning crisis into opportunity. The challenges we face today are a clarion-call to change the way we think about seeds.

> Ordinary farmers and gardeners created the world's abundant diversity, the fields from which agriculture first emerged. Now it is up to farmers and gardeners to save it.

The barriers to food security and self-reliance are imposing, corporate and international. The hegemonic seed giants have considerable sway over legislation to protect their interests and have won favor in the courts. Yet as desperate as it seems, there is still hope. We can save our way out of this. We can save our own seeds. Ordinary farmers and gardeners created the world's abundant diversity, the fields from which agriculture first emerged. Now it is up to farmers and gardeners to save it. Our common sense interaction with our immediate environment—and the unlimited potential in each seed—offers us our best chance to survive and to thrive. It always has. One farmer, one gardener, one field or garden at a time.

To Learn More

Organic Seed Alliance (OSA)
PO Box 772, Port Townsend, WA 98368. 360-385-7192
www.seedalliance.org
Education through publications and workshops, research though participatory plant breeding projects with farmers, consulting with direct technical assistance.

Seed School, Native Seeds/S.E.A.R.C.H.
P.O. Box 596 Cornville, AZ 86325. 928-649-3315 Fax:
877.686.7524; www.seedstrust.com; bell@seedstrust.com

Teaches practical, detailed information necessary to recreate the genetic foundation for a truly sustainable agriculture.

Books:
Principles of Plant Breeding, Robert Allard, Wiley, 2nd Edition, 1999.
Breed Your Own Vegetable Varieties, Carol Deppe, Chelsea Green; 2nd edition, 2000.
The Resilient Gardener: Food Production and Self-Reliance in Uncertain Times, Carol Deppe, Chelsea Green Publishing; 1st edition, 2010.
Seed to Seed: Seed Saving and Growing Techniques for Vegetable Gardeners, Suzanne Ashworth and Kent Whealy, Seed Savers Exchange; 2nd edition, 2002.
Basic Seed Saving, Bill McDorman, Seeds Trust, 1994.
Return to Resistance: Breeding Crops to Reduce Pesticide Dependence, R. Robinson, IDRC Books, 1995.

[**Editor's Note:** This article first appeared in *Acres Magazine*, January 11, 2011 edition.]

❖ SPIELARTS PUBLICATION DESIGN

❖ SITE-RITE WEB DESIGN

Book / Magazine & Website design
Illustration, Graphic design, Fine art

www.site-rite.net
719.630.7324

www.spielarts.com
paul@spielarts.com

TOOLS AND TALENT TO BRING YOUR VISION INTO REALITY

Aspen
by Kim Gravestock

A Sex in the Garden Essay

by Elisabeth Kinsey

Beguiling the Poppy

I never knew I could be the sort of woman who grew poppies. These women live in gigantic houses with terraced gardens, boasting dripping sedum and perfect bunches of perennials, color coded, tendrilling out of their hibernation in perfect cycles. These women, some sturdy with spiky hair, licking their girlfriend's ear in public, some in long overall-type dresses, tight curly hair never getting into their eyes, their hunky husbands, sporting tool belts, bursting out of the house with a glass of wine on a golden tray. "Honey, why don't you leave the garden for now?"

These women don't sweat. These women hold the secret to the California poppies' papery orange ecstatic fluttering, the virgin pink or dragon-red flames of corn poppies grouping around the walkway. These poppy women are able to survey their bursting gardens from a flagstoned patio glance, while sipping their Nebbiolo or Chenin Blanc. These women were not me. I tried to grow poppies and failed.

A Colorado master gardener friend (I'll call her Camille) pshawed this idea. "Beth," she said, "Your problem is that you want to coddle your plants. You can't think of poppies as if they're roses. You need to be like a dude and ignore them. You need to play hard to get."

Could it be that I was overanalyzing the poppy? Expert gardener Barbara Pleasant claims the poppy to be the "easiest plant to grow." She writes, "You can grow them in Sleetmute, Alaska. You can grow them in Corkscrew, Florida. Heck, there was even a big patch of them just shy of Oz on the Yellow Brick Road!" Was I the only gardener around who had bad luck growing

poppies? To understand the poppy, I had to get into poppy-mind. Not to plunge into its aphrodisiac qualities (we're not allowed to grow that variety here), but to understand its wants and needs. Basically, Camille had me pegged. I was an overbearing drudge. Poppies held a grudge against me.

To lure this beauty from my sandy acidic soil, I had to stop planting it in the "normal" planting seasons. As I read up on this obstinate beauty, I learned what's obvious to me now. Don't grow this seed indoors with your herbs in February. Don't even let its papery folds, its furry bulb head into your mind in the spring. No. This plant needs to be ignored, left alone. Which is so hard for me. Look at *Le Coquelicot* (yes, the root of this name is *Coq*) by Kees Van Dongen (and now ignore the *dong* in Dongen). It's the over exaggerated red hat, the woman's eyes looking off away from its viewer, confidant of the action she'll be getting momentarily. The poppy is a primal need. This is what it feels like to be human.

Camille commanded, "Throw those poppy seeds on the cold ground and then they'll want your love."

Camille commanded, "Throw those poppy seeds on the cold ground and then they'll want your love." I didn't even have to prepare my soil. When I was able to let go of this idea of seducing these almost-alien-at-first bodies out of my inadequate garden patch, it was almost too much for me. Nothing to coddle, watch under grow lights, no spring grace during winter in my living room, where I was all-knowing, all-seeing grower.

Poppies are actinomorphic, not zygomorphic, which according to Ushimaru et al means that in the world of flower sex is "easily pollinated." Poppies throw themselves freely to any honey bee coming along to plunge into their open folds. To the sluts of the floral world, I was coming on too strong.

I took my *Papaver rhoeas* seeds when the wind held enough chill for me to feel like eating lentil soup and wearing slippers all day and threw them onto the cold ground in the corner of my garden where I had previously tried planting something fluttering and pink. Yes. Then they came. The poppies rose up and out in a mild May, furry, wanton, curving bundles, obstinate, and soon to throw open color into my landscape.

Throw those poppy seeds onto the ground unabashedly. They need nothing more. Do this, and you'll have the poppy's heart forever. We can all be this sort of woman. ✿

Le Coquelicot ("The Corn Poppy"), by Kees Van Dongen, 1919

References:

Ushimaru, Atushi, Ikumi Dohzono, Yasuoki Takami, and Fujio Hyodo. 2009. "Flower orientation enhances pollen transfer in bilaterally symmetrical flowers." Oecologia 160, no. 4: 667-674. Academic Search Premier, EBSCOhost (accessed February 7, 2011).
Pleasant, Barbara. 1995. "Poppies make the world go round." Organic Gardening (08973792) 42, no. 5: 68. GreenFILE, EBSCOhost (accessed February 7, 2011).

Butterflies and Poppies, Vincent van Gogh

Hello Doobie Tuesday

A Visit to a Boulder, Colorado, Medical Marijuana Dispensary
by Pat Cook Gulya
(Art by Kristian Angel)

Walking through the glass door under the words "Helping Hands Herbals," printed on a giant marijuana leaf picture, we entered a space that looked like a doctor's office waiting room. The doormat rang out, announcing our entrance, and I stood awkwardly beside my stepdaughter, Bea, and my husband, Dale. On one side of the room was a counter strewn with official looking documents, and, behind it, a desk sporting the usual desktop accoutrements. A white board on the wall listed "Daily Specials" and beside it hung a giant framed poster of two goldfish.

No one appeared, so we sat on a couch next to a table piled with free magazines: *Marijuana Times*, *West Coast Cannabis*, and *A Patient's Guide to Colorado Dispensaries*.

Across from us a one-hundred gallon aquarium served as a wall. Swimming slowly in the aquarium were two huge angelfish and a goldfish that could have posed for the poster on the wall. As Pink Floyd's "Dark Side of the Moon," wafted through the rooms from ceiling speakers, I peered through the aquarium water into a back room where several people sat on another couch.

What a difference, I thought, remembering the darkened, smoke-filled living rooms of the 1960s where the furniture was mainly floor pillows. Entry into those spaces, usually in older parts of town with minimal house upkeep, occurred by saying something like, "I'm a friend of Dave's and he said to tell you hi."

While Bea and Dale talked quietly, I leafed through *West Coast Cannabis* and skimmed an article called "Getting High with Dragonfly." Dragonfly, a columnist for the magazine, sampled a different brand of cannabis each month and evaluated it. In this issue, she reported on Dr. Walker's Dose, which she said was so good that her companion put his hoodie on upside down, so the hood covered his butt.

As I turned to the centerfold, a 10" marijuana bud, I noticed identical ads printed on pages 43 and 80. I wondered if the editor, or perhaps the advertiser, was sampling Dr. Walker's Dose along with Dragonfly.

The door next to the aquarium opened and a twenty-something young man wearing jeans and a bright yellow t-shirt walked through the waiting area, nodding to us as he exited. I looked over a recipe for mac and cheese using marijuana butter. It sounded appetizing, certainly could add some zing to a bland dish. Many of the marijuana ads stressed, "It's Organic" to convince people that it is healthy. But the important thing to me is that marijuana is not physically addictive like prescription painkillers.

Across the room stood a showcase displaying apothecary-type jars containing large marijuana buds with names like: Kryptonite, Blue Moonshine, Big Fatty, King Kush and Sour Diesel. A small bowl on the counter contained several joints. The sign on the bowl said "Free."

A few minutes later, another young male customer, wearing shorts and sandals, exited without looking in our direction. It was ten more minutes before a man with graying hair, wearing a flannel shirt, appeared from the back.

"Oh, hello," he said, looking surprised to see us. "It looks like we are busy." He sized us up. "Two of you need services?" He looked at Bea, a scarf covering her bald head, then glanced at me, I'm not sure why, maybe because of the resemblance between Dale and his daughter.

"Oh no, just one." Bea stood and walked to his desk, carrying the certificate her doctor gave her that morning when she got her semi-weekly dose of chemotherapy to fight her breast cancer. It took her two weeks to convince him to give her the documentation she needed to purchase medical marijuana. She didn't have to pay the fee for her certificate like most people, since she is on Medicaid.

"I'm Mike," the man shook Bea's hand then explained that the state had a backlog of paperwork to process and they were very slow. "It may take four months to get your card," he said, "but you can purchase from us now. Do you want to make us your caregiver?"

"Do I need to decide that today?" Bea asked.

"Oh no, but we'd like to be your caregiver," Mike pressed.

"I'm not ready to do that."

I'd heard that in order to stay in business each dispensary has to have a certain number of patients name them as their caregiver.

"Be sure to make copies of anything you send into the state," Mike said. "They've been losing people's forms frequently. Come on back."

Dale and I followed Bea through the door next to the aquarium. Directly behind the aquarium were the couches I'd spied through the water, set up in an *U*, with a coffee table in the middle. This space was larger than the front.

As I looked around, I tried to maintain an air of interest mixed with nonchalance. I'd consumed my share of weed but stopped indulging over twenty years ago. I've found alternative ways to achieve feelings of bliss: meditation, yoga and bicycling. I believe that adults should be allowed to self-medicate and that doctors should be free to prescribe whatever works to relieve discomfort and suffering. In 2000, I was one of the 54% of Coloradoans that voted to make marijuana legal for medical use.

Across the room stood a showcase displaying apothecary-type jars containing large marijuana buds with names like: Kryptonite, Blue Moonshine, Big Fatty, King Kush and Sour Diesel. A small bowl on the counter contained several joints. The sign on the bowl said "Free."

On an adjacent wall, several small healthy-looking marijuana plants with three sets of leaves grew on a metal stand, basking in light from a grow lamp. An attached sign read "Clones." The plants looked healthy and I resisted looking at them more closely.

In the 60s, when the government began spraying paraquat on concealed marijuana crops, I started growing my own. I think they are very pretty plants and fun to grow.

An ice cream freezer stood across from the display case. A sign on the top listed several flavors, all created by "Mile High Ice Cream": Brown Sugar Pot Tart, Chocolate

Peanut Butter, Boulder Brownie and several others. Four-inch square brownies were displayed on a table next to individually wrapped greenish cookies.

A lady with flowing hair and a long skirt, about Bea's age, in her forties, appeared. "I'm Donna, what can I help you find?" She assisted Bea while Dale stood near the couch, looking uncomfortable and bored.

"Eating marijuana is different than smoking; it takes longer to 'kick in' but lasts longer," Donna said. "The leaves are used for edibles, cooked down in butter or oil then squeezed. The buds are for smoking."

In the 60s we smoked it all. The typical bag had leaves, stems, seeds and an occasional bud or two. Some crushed it all but others picked out the good parts leaving the stems and seeds for last. This practice resulted in songs about being down to "Stems and Seeds." The only edibles then were Alice B. Toklas Brownies, which contained any and all plant-parts—in abundance. Lots of nuts were included to hide the crunchiness.

While Bea was deciding what she wanted to try, a thirty-something man wearing casual business attire entered and peered through the glass at the jars of buds, examining them carefully. His purchase, one ounce, cost $300.00, which he paid for with a card.

Bea chose three ½-pint containers of ice cream and a brownie. Donna suggested that she only eat half of the container initially to gauge the effect. Each ice cream cost $10.00 and the brownies were $10.00 each.

On the drive back to Bea's house, she said she'd only tried pot once or twice and hadn't been impressed. We speculated about the preponderance of young men, in their twenties and thirties, visiting the dispensary. Are there that many sick young men? Or are the ailing men in that age group drawn to using medical marijuana? Of course, we didn't know the answers but media coverage hinted that some doctors were supplying Colorado Medical Marijuana Registry ID cards to anyone who asked.

We joked about Boulder recently being named, "The Happiest City in the USA" by *USA Today*. I suggested that was because it has the most dispensaries in Colorado, a fact that I noticed while looking through the "Guide to Colorado Dispensaries."

Later Bea napped and Dale played the guitar, while I read magazines from the clinic to learn more about marijuana. There are two major types of cannabis plants: *Indica*, (*Cannabis sativa indica*) and *Sativa*, (*Cannabis sativa sativa*.) They look different and have different qualities. Indica is a shorter, bushier plant, originally from hashish-producing countries of the world like Afghanistan, Morocco and Tibet. The *indica*'s high, described as a pleasant body buzz, is great for relaxation, stress relief, insomnia and for overall body pain.

Sativa provides a spacey high but keeps one more alert, so it's better for daytime use. The effects of *sativa* marijuana are cerebral, providing feelings of optimism and well-being. *Sativas* smell sweeter than the skunky indicas.

Some of the marijuana brands are hybrids of both types, creating a desired blockage for the patient's pain, be it physical, or anxiety-related, like Post Traumatic Stress Disorder.

The popular varieties in the 60s were Acapulco Gold and Panama Red, and I wondered what type they had been.

Later that evening, Bea decided to eat some of the triple chocolate brownie, provocatively named "*Ménage au trois*." She broke off and nibbled a small piece, seeming to be afraid of the possible effects. She offered some to us, but we declined. Were I to come down with a physical situation for which marijuana use would make me more comfortable, I wouldn't hesitate to use it.

Wednesday morning, while drinking coffee and reading the *Boulder Weekly*, I noticed an advertisement saying that Tuesday is Doobie Tuesday at "Helping Hand Herbals" and each customer gets a free joint with a purchase. Bea didn't get a free joint but maybe that's because she only purchased edibles or because she didn't ask.

At breakfast, she said she didn't know if eating the brownie helped her sleep better. Later on, she tried the ice cream, but ended up relying on the pharmaceuticals prescribed by her doctor to control the side effects of her treatments.

However, numerous people rely on medical marijuana to help them sustain a pain-free life. Bea's grandmother (my mother-in-law) suffered for years with pain from shingles. Her doctor suggested that marijuana might ease her pain. This was in the 1990s, before any states had medical marijuana and she didn't have a source, but I will always wonder if her last few years would have been more enjoyable if she could have sipped some marijuana tea mid-morning, or had a dish of Boulder Brownie ice cream before bedtime.

Like every substance, THC, the active ingredient in marijuana, affects each person differently; some people get very anxious or paranoid, others just want to sleep. Therefore, medical marijuana isn't for everyone, but I feel proud to live in a state where people are becoming open-minded enough to let doctors heal people and control suffering.

Postscript: Bea's breast cancer responded favorably to treatments, meaning that the tumor shrunk and was then surgically removed. At last report, she was cancer-free, but still recovering from the ordeal.

Medical Marijuana in the U.S. Today

Fourteen states and Washington DC have legalized medical marijuana. The states include: Colorado, Alaska, California, Hawaii, Maine, Michigan, Montana, Nevada, New Jersey, New Mexico, Oregon, Rhode Island, Vermont and Washington. California was the first state in 1996 and most recent are New Jersey and DC in 2010. Arizona allows physicians to prescribe MM and Maryland allows medical-use defense in court.❃

Lemon Kush by Kristian Angel

Statistics for Colorado medical marijuana recipients:

Gender	Percentage	Average age
Male	74%	39
Female	26%	42

Reported Condition	No. of Patients	Percentage
Cachexia	700	2%
Cancer	908	2%
Glaucoma	382	1%
HIV/AIDS	296	1%
Muscle Spasms	12,077	29%
Seizures	764	2%
Severe Pain	37,912	92%
Severe Nausea	6,696	16%

Source: http://www.cdphe.state.co.us/hs/medicalmarijuana/statistics.html

MEN AT WORK

by Maureen S. Fry

So what's the story with men and mowers?
Front lawns scalped within an inch of their lives.
The highway medians' goldenrod and daisies
beheaded where they stand. Along country roads,
armies of grasses cut down, fallen
in orderly ranks behind the sickle bar.
Some guys use a bush hog; it cuts a swath
five feet wide, slices through saplings
the size of my wrist.

Question: How many bush hogs does it take
to down a rainforest?

Then there's all that oiling, sharpening,
polishing, until the machine gleams
in its corner of the garage, ready
for any emergency. Who knows when
some strip of green might go berserk?
(I know a man who mowed down his family
garden when a mob of thistles overran
the pepper plants.)

And as for those devils that escape the blade—
running down slopes, huddled at the base
of trees, bunched against a fence—bring on
the weed whacker; hack them to pieces.

CREATURE FEATURE

by DB Rudin

THE GARDEN ASSASSIN

Mantis drawing by Rachael Davis, Collage by Sandra Knauf

Of all the potential insect visitors gardeners may encounter, perhaps none has more charisma than the Praying Mantis. "The ultimate insect assassin" is how famed British filmmaker David Attenborough describes it. You can forgive Sir David a bit of hyperbole when you realize that this is the only insect in the world with a martial arts style modeled after it, Praying Mantis Kung Fu.

The story goes that one Wang Lang, a Taoist monk in 17th century, Ming Dynasty era China, was resting in the shade of a willow tree on a hot summer's day. There he observed a praying mantis defeat a larger cicada by using skill rather than mere force. Intrigued, the young monk captured the mantis and enticed (the word *badgered* comes to mind) the mantis into sparring by poking at him with the handle of his writing brush. Wang Lang learned that the mantis had a definite style, even a certain panache. It used techniques like weaving, advancing, retreating and grasping. No record exists whether or not other martial artists snickered under their breath when Wang shared his discovery. After all, other martial arts styles were modeled after cranes, snakes, leopards, tigers and even dragons. Here was Wang looking to a—well, to a bug—for inspiration.

One could easily argue, however, that the fighting style of the mantis is only one intriguing aspect of this insect. Perhaps not even its most remarkable. For starters, the praying mantis isn't a single species but rather the common name for a vast complex of species totaling over 2,000 and counting. The "praying" part of the name comes from those amazing raptorial forelegs. Armed with spikes for holding onto prey, they are often held up in front of the head as if our little friend is deep in prayer. In fact, the European mantis's scientific name is *Mantis religiosa.*

The mantis' religious bent goes beyond prayer, as the name *mantis* comes from the Greek word for prophet and much folklore is associated with it. For example, an old European folktale holds that they help wayward children find their way home. A Muslim tale says that mantises always pray facing Mecca.

Some have argued that all this religious symbolism is beside the point and they should be called "preying" mantis to reflect their role as fearsome hunters of prey. For, while there is considerable variability among species, there are no vegetarians in their ranks. Amongst the many species found around the world are a tremendous variety of sizes and camouflage strategies. When full grown, mantises range from easy-to-miss half-inch long sprites to 7 ½" bruisers fully capable of taking out small birds, mice, frogs and even snakes. Wang Lang was on to something when he created his style of martial art. These aren't bugs to be underestimated.

Mantises are more than mere fighting brutes. Like ninja assassins, they are masters of disguise. They are able to hide in plain sight, looking like dead leaves, sticks, grass, blotchy green and white tree bark, and perhaps, most famously, flowers. Some of the loveliest imitate orchids. Their pink and white bodies disappear among the leaves. This allows them to hide from would-be predators as well as potential prey. Throughout the U. S., you are often more likely to run into non-native mantises, known as "adventives," with brown or green coloration.

Adventives are introduced or escaped non-native species that are now self-sustaining in the wild. Most U. S. adventives are Chinese and European mantises. Introduced from abroad to help control insect pest populations, they are now ubiquitous throughout the country. Their egg cases, or *oothecae*, are commonly available from garden supply companies for insect control. So, should one take the plunge and buy some mantis egg cases for the garden? In a word, maybe.

When a mantis egg case (usually it is the Chinese mantis that is sold) hatches out, a small army of newborn mantises are born, each a miniature replica of an adult. As is common in nature, far more offspring are born than will survive to adulthood. As they grow to adult size they have to shed, or molt, their exoskeleton as many as seven or more times. The ultimate molt means adulthood and two significant bonuses—sexual maturity and wings. The males take advantage of their wings, flying at night in search of females. The females, heavily laden with eggs, use their wings more sparingly. In some species the females' wings are reduced in size or absent altogether. Throughout their lives they will employ their formidable hunting skills to capture and

Mantises are quite capable of plucking house flies out of mid-air; in fact, they routinely do.

eat whatever they can grasp with those signature spiked forelegs: pests and pollinators. They don't discriminate.

As most gardeners know, there are no easy fixes when it comes to combating insect pests. Because of the mantis' refusal to be more accommodating and eat only pests, they are no silver bullet. However, there is nothing quite like watching a mantis swaying side to side, judging distance by seeing how its potential prey moves against a backdrop, and then striking in a flash. Mantises are quite capable of plucking house flies out of mid-air; in fact, they routinely do.

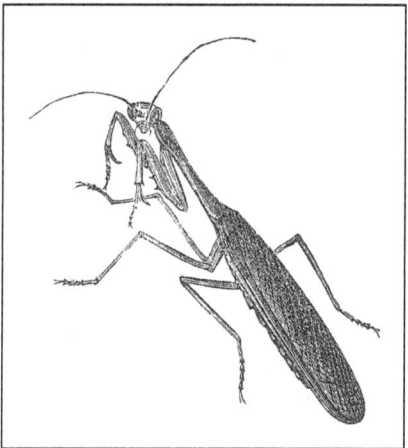

No amount of mantis acrobatics will allow them to out-maneuver and survive winter. But if you are lucky, you will have at least one adult female that will mate and lay egg cases for next year. These oothecae are indeed able to survive the winter. Bringing them inside or in a greenhouse won't necessarily work as they need a cooling down period and moisture to successfully hatch. Best to let Mother Nature handle this.

Whether or not they possess supernatural powers, the mantis continues to fascinate, and they are worth an up-close viewing. Even the largest females can be handled if you gently encourage them to walk up onto your hand. Rough handling might be met with an impressive defensive display, wings open, forelegs spread out. Grabbing might injure the mantis, and beware, they have no reservations about pinching or biting if the intruding human continues to play rough. So the next time you make a casual visit to your garden, keep your wits about you. Lurking invisibly amongst the tomato plants might be a cold-blooded killer, ninja assassin, prophet and even occasionally a gardeners' ally—all rolled into one. ✳

The Scoville Heat Index of You

by D'Arcy Fallon

(Wilbur Scoville developed a scale in 1912 to measure the heat in chilies.)

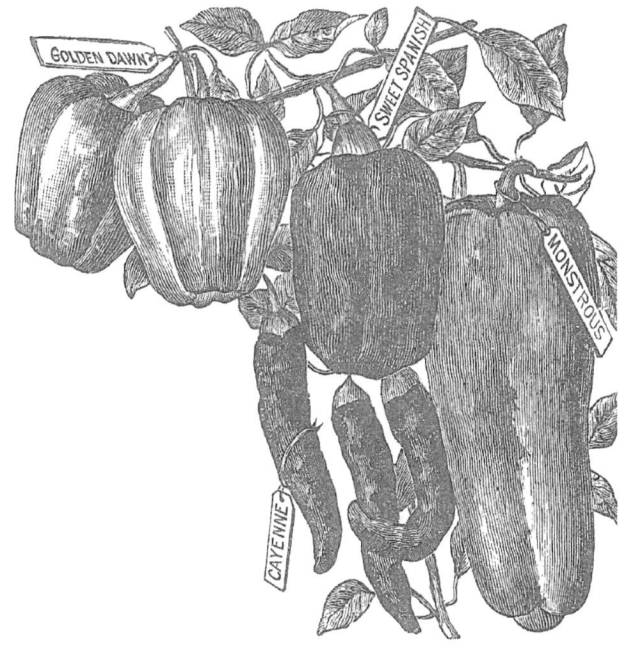

All I want is peppers. Poblanos that dial up

endorphins, serranos that scald the heart,

smoldering jalapenos to surf on, past

the breakwater of no return.

The heat is in the veins

and also in the seeds.

My tongue tingles.

Biting you,

I burn.

"We are all interconnected." -- Sir Jagadish Chandra Bose

Indian Plant Guru

by Sandra Knauf

Do you think plants can feel? This scientist proved many years ago that indeed they can.—Ed.

The setting is a grand lecture hall in the Royal Society of London in the Victorian era. An audience of scientists and scholars is awash in murmurs over what they've just seen.

Sitting on the lecture table are unusual metal instruments. They include something called a Crescograph: a mechanical recording device created by the visiting scientist. Journalist F. Yeats-Brown, who is there for *The Spectator*, writes that the device magnifies "so inconceivably that the pace of a snail would become eight times faster than a bullet." Nearby is a potted mimosa plant under artificial lights.

Yeats-Brown takes notes on what will be cabled as a "modern miracle of science." The world will be "startled" to learn that Sir Jagadish Chandra Bose, the Indian biologist, has demonstrated, in the presence of this learned audience, that a plant has a "heart," which acts physiologically very much as a heart does in the animal kingdom.

Bose had described the mimosa earlier saying, "This poor little plant is rather depressed, and no wonder. But it's alive in spite of your climate, and so I shall be able to show you its nerve impulses and its reactions to various drugs."

The audience watches as Bose takes a pair of scissors and cuts a branch from the mimosa. He inserts it into his recording machine. A needle pierces the branch's skin.

The audience witnesses the plant's pulsations, like heart-beats, magnified a "million fold," on a wall projection.

Bose explains, "The pulse will grow fainter and fainter, of course, as it bleeds to death."

The audience stares at the spot of light that illustrates the "death-struggle" of the plant. The pulsations grow slower and weaker, then stop, just as predicted.

"Of course!" writes Yeats-Brown.

Earlier, the audience had witnessed Bose as he administered a little bromide into the plant, which almost caused its death. Then he injected an extract of thyroid, which made for "skittish" readings, then, finally, the cobra venom, which produced a stimulus, then the death-pang.

The implications of Bose's discoveries? In the words of Yeats-Brown: "Carrots can get drunk and write the scrawling story of their dissipation. Plants tell Sir Jagadis [sic] how they feel when he shocks them with a loud noise; fat ones feel it less than their more slender and sensitive sisters."

An amazing revelation, that plants feel and react very much like we do.

Sir Jagadish Chandra Bose is best known as one of the founding fathers of radio science. His demonstration of remote wireless signaling predated Marconi's, and he was a pioneer in the investigation of radio waves. His discoveries and inventions were many, including the design of an instrument in 1897 which generated very short electrical waves (measured in millimeters) when others were struggling with Hertzian electric waves that were about three meters long. Bose was also the first to use a semi-conducting crystal as a detection of radio waves, and he invented various microwave components that are in common use today.

Bose was what is known as a polymath (someone with knowledge of many subjects). Aside from being one of the fathers of radio science, he was a physicist, biologist, botanist, archeologist and the father of Bengali science fiction. But what may be most fascinating to those of us with an interest in botany is Bose's discoveries into plant life. He was the first to proclaim, "We are all interconnected."

Bose was born on the 30th of November, 1858, in Rarikhal, Bengal, India. His father was a civil servant who rebelled against the standard children's education of that time for someone of his rank in society—he chose not to send his children to an English school for their early education, which was expected. Instead, he insisted his children learn first among their own people. In a vernacular school, young Jagadish studied his native language and culture among children whom, in his words, were the progeny of those "who tilled the ground and made the land blossom with green verdure and

> "Carrots can get drunk and write the scrawling story of their dissipation. Plants tell Sir Jagadis [sic] how they feel when he shocks them with a loud noise; fat ones feel it less than their more slender and sensitive sisters."

ripening corn, and the sons of the fisher folk." From his country's literature he became familiar with the great epics, and from his fellow students he drew his love of nature. This early experience would forge a strong bond to his culture, and Bose would remain closely connected to his people.

His education continued in Xavier's Collegiate School in Calcutta, the Calcutta University, and finally

There were no secrets as to the construction of his inventions, and he did not use the patents granted to him for personal gain. He declared that his work was, "open to all the world to adopt for practical and money-making purpose."

at Christ's College in Cambridge, England. He earned two science degrees. He also earned a Bachelor of Science degree from the University of London in 1884. In 1885, he became an officiating Professor of Physical Science at the Presidency College in Calcutta. There, being an Indian and an officiating Professor, he was allowed to only draw one-third of his pay grade. In protest, Bose refused to accept any salary for three years. After those three years he was appointed to Professor and received a pay increase of double his prior salary (which was still only two-thirds the pay of European professors) as well as the three years back pay. He would not receive an equal wage for 18 more years.

This, however, was only one of many challenges he'd face. Unlike his American and European counterparts, Professor Bose did not have an appropriate laboratory in which to work. His facilities consisted of a 24 square-foot room and he received only the help of one untrained tinsmith to assist in constructing research equipment. Research was done on his own time and with his own money. Nevertheless, within a decade Bose emerged as a pioneer in the developing research field of wireless radio waves.

In recognition of his many contributions during this decade, the University of London conferred on him the Degree of Doctor of Science, and in 1896, the Cambridge University awarded him the degree of M.A. The Royal Institution of Great Britain invited him to deliver a 'Friday Evening Discourse' on his work, which was

considered a privilege and the highest distinction that could be bestowed on a man of science.

Bose met Guglielmo Marconi in 1896, at least a year before Marconi conducted his wireless signaling experiment on Salisbury Plain, and a year after Bose conducted his public demonstrating of remote wireless signaling in Kolkata (Calcutta). Later, in an interview, Bose expressed disinterest in commercial telegraphy and made it known that others were welcome to use his research work. In 1904 he was the first from the Indian subcontinent to get a U.S. patent, for his invention of a certain crystal receiver which proved to be the most sensitive detector of the wireless signal. There were no secrets as to the construction of his inventions, and he did not use the patents granted to him for personal gain. He declared that his work was, "open to all the world to adopt for practical and money-making purpose." He was quoted in the Calcutta magazine *Modern Review* as saying, "The spirit of our national culture demands that we should for ever be free from the desecration of utilizing knowledge for personal gain."

According to another article in *Modern Review* it was during this time, while he researching radio waves and materials used for receivers, that Bose became interested in the response of other materials, namely metals and plants. "[Bose] found that the uncertainty of the early type of his receiver was brought on by 'fatigue' and that the curve of fatigue of his [metal] instrument closely resembled the fatigue curve of animal muscle." This spurred him to further experiments, and he soon saw that the fatigue of his instrument was removed by suitable stimulants. In addition, he found that application of certain poisons permanently eradicated the instrument's sensitiveness. He was amazed at this discovery—this parallelism in the behavior of the 'receiver' material to the living muscle tissue of animals. This led him to a systematic study of all matter, organic and inorganic, living and non-living.

Universal Response

Dr. Bose began to research how metals reacted to stimulus in a full range of experiments—mechanical, thermal, chemical and electrical. He found that each stimulus produced a measurable electric response. This led him to try the same stimulus in plants and animal tissues, and he found, again, the same results. All materials —metals, plant tissues, and animal tissues, were affected in the same ways. In his book, *Response in the Living and Non-Living*, Dr. Bose wrote that the materials were "benumbed by cold, intoxicated by alcohol, fatigued by excessive work, stupefied by anesthetics, excited by electric currents, stung by physical blows and killed by poison—they all exhibit essentially the same phenomena of fatigue and depression, together with possibilities of recovery and exaltation, yet also that of permanent irresponsiveness which is associated with death—they are all responsive or irresponsive under the same conditions and in the same manner." This finding is what Dr. Bose termed "universal response."

Dr. Bose wrote a paper on his findings in 1900, and on June 5, 1901 he presented a demonstration to the Royal Society "On Electric Response of Inorganic Substances." Immediately, he was met with objections and strong criticism, particularly from Sir John Burden Sanderson (the leading physiologist) and his followers who attacked him on the belief that a physicist should not be straying into the work of physiologists. Bose's paper was not published but placed in the archives. A *Modern Review* article revealed how another paper, published in another journal by another Society, eight months later, was found to be a plagiarism of Dr. Bose's work and led to "much unpleasantness." The article also stated that "the determined hostility and misrepresentation of one man succeeded for more than 10 years to bar all avenues of publications for his [Bose's] discoveries."

The end result of all this would be that Bose would work for the next decade to prove his research was valid.

In March 1902, he performed a series of experiments before the Linnean Society showing electric response in plants when subjected to fatigue, temperature changes, poisons and anesthetics. Again, the responses were identical with those seen in animal muscle and nerve tissue. In June 1902 he wrote a paper, "On the Electric Response in Animal, Vegetable, and Metal."

While Dr. Bose used the *Mimosa pudica* plant (now known as "sensitivity plant") for his experiments to most easily demonstrate his findings, he made it clear in his book *On Electric Response of Ordinary Plants Under Mechanical Stimulus* that "all plants are sensitive." He went on to demonstrate that not only every plant, but every part of every plant exhibited an electric response to stimulus. ". . . all plants, even the trees, are fully alive to changes of environment; they respond visibly to all stimuli, even to the slight fluctuations of light by a drifting cloud."

> " . . . all plants, even the trees, are fully alive to changes of environment; they respond visibly to all stimuli, even to the slight fluctuations of light by a drifting cloud."

'Tropic' Movements," Ascent of Sap," and "Growth"

Dr. Bose found that plants gave not only electric responses to stimulus but response through movement (also called tropic or motive response) which could be measured. These movements, however, were extremely diverse. Light, for example, sometimes induced a positive curvature in plant tissue, sometimes a negative one. Gravitation induced one movement in the root, and the opposition in the shoot. Other movements, not outwardly visible, could also be measured. Growth and the ascent of sap, for example, were shown to be reactions to outward stimulus. This may now seem simplistic, especially to gardeners who are used to thinking in these terms, but viewing plants as connected and perceptive life forms and researching this through scientific means was new at that time. Bose invented a machine called the Shoshungraph that measured the ascent of sap and a growth recorder, or Balanced Crescograph, that determined the influences of various agencies on growth. The instruments were so finely created that they could measure real growth within a few seconds, and measure the response of a plant to a fertilizer, food, poison, electrical current, or other stimulants in less than fifteen minutes.

Plant Sleep and "Death Spasms"

Dr. Bose showed that there is no physical response in the most highly organized animal tissue that does not also occur within the plant. His "Researches on Diurnal Sleep" showed that plants react with different intensity depending upon whether it is day or night, and that there is a periodic insensibility in both plants and animals that correspond to what we call sleep. Furthermore, plants' responses matched animals' in comparison to what time of day they become alert. By tracking reaction on an impulse through all hours of a day, Bose found that a plant "wakes up during morning slowly, becomes fully alert by noon, and becomes sleepy only after midnight, resembling man in a surprising manner."

Dr. Bose also showed that plants undergo a "death spasm," at the time of death, that is the same as in animals'.

On January 1, 1917, in recognition of his important scientific work, the English government conferred on him a Knighthood. This was the first time that this honor had been given to an Indian.

He invented an instrument (Morograph) with which he recorded the critical point of death of a plant.

He also demonstrated that there is an essential unity regarding the effects of drugs on plant and animal tissues and that the effects were determined by the individual plant or animal's "constitution" (size, strength, health, etc.).

In 1903 Dr. Bose presented research papers to the Royal Society on "Investigation on Mechanical Response in Plants," "On Polar Effects of Currents on the Stimulation of Plants," and five other related topics.

These new contributions were seen as important by the Royal Society, and the papers were recommended to be published in the Society's Philosophical Transactions. However, opposition was once again raised and publication ultimately withheld. The Royal Society stated that while Dr. Bose's discoveries were important they were also so unexpected and so contrary to existing theories that the choice was made to reserve judgment on the research until at some future time when the plants themselves could be made to record their answers to questions put to them. This stipulation was interpreted by some as the final rejection of Dr. Bose's theories. Worse still, the support which he was relying on for his research was in danger of being withdrawn.

Undeterred, Bose directed his attention to a single goal—how to reveal the plants' reactions by means of their own "autographs."

In Dr. Bose's book, *Comparative Electro-physiology: A Physico-Physiological Study*, he stated that plants, like animals, were single organic wholes, all parts interconnected, their activities coordinated by "conducting strands" which we call in animals, nerves. Positive and negative responses, pleasure and pain, could be deter-

mined in all organisms.

Again, Dr. Bose was treading new ground. His view on the function of nerves was seen as alarming —"causing the dividing frontiers between Physics, Physiology, and Psychology to disappear." At this time nerves were universally regarded as typically non-motile (or incapable of movement), and their responses were believed to be characteristically different from those of muscle. Bose showed that nerves were indeed motile and similar to muscle in their responses; through experiment he showed that the isolated vegetal nerve was indistinguishable from that of animal nerve.

It took years for Dr. Bose to design the supersensitive instruments and apparatus which would make it possible to show plant response—"by means of their own autographs." His "Resonant and Oscillating Recorders" gave a simple and direct method of obtaining a record. "The plant by its self-made records, showed exultation with alcohol, depression with chloroform, rapid transmission of a shock with the application of heat, and an abolition of the propagated impulse with the application of a deadly poison like potassium cyanide. This variation in the transmitted impulse, under physiological variations, showed that it was not a physical one."

Royal Society

Dr. Bose had achieved what had seemed impossible, creating a mechanism that would enable a plant to tell its own story through records made by its reactions. Through the convincing character of the demonstrations that he gave with his Resonant Recorder and other delicate instruments, leading Scientific Societies became convinced, and Dr. Bose soon secured a worldwide acceptance of his theories and results. The Royal Society could no longer withhold recognition and his paper "On an Automatic Method, for the Investigation of the Velocity of Transmission of Excitation in Mimosa" was published in the *Philosophical Transactions of the Royal Society* in 1913.

In 1911 Dr. Bose was awarded the insignia of the Companion of the Order of the Star of India by His

Majesty the King Emperor and The Calcutta University conferred the honorary Doctor of Science degree to him. In 1913 he published the book *Researches on Irritability of Plants*, and by 1915 he had received hundreds of invitations to speak throughout the United States.

"The very convincing character of the demonstrations that he gave, before the leading Scientific Societies of the world, with his newly invented Resonant Recorder and other delicate instruments, secured a worldwide acceptance of his theories and results."

On January 1, 1917, in recognition of his important scientific work, the English government conferred on him a Knighthood. This was the first time that this honor had been given to an Indian.

Later that year, on his 60th birthday (November 30), Sir Jagadish realized a dream that he'd had for many years. He founded the Bose Institute in India. Here students could study the inhabitants of a garden—plants, vines, trees and more—in their natural environment. Here, according to the *Presidency College Magazine*, "the student would watch the panorama of life" and "isolated from all distractions, would learn to attune himself with nature and to see how community throughout the great ocean of life outweighs apparent the dissimilarity." Opening this institution of learning, which he dedicated to the Nation, for the progress of Science and for the Glory of India, took Sir Jagadish's entire life savings.

The aims of the Institute were clear. An article in *Modern Review* stated that there would be no academic limitation to the widest possible diffusion of knowledge. The facilities of the Institute would be available to workers from all countries and there would be no desecration of knowledge by its utilization for personal gain; in other words, no patents would be taken of the discoveries made there. This "great Seat of Learning" would be maintained through those means and by presenting lectures that were not second-hand knowledge repeated but lectures focused on new discoveries announced to the world for the first time.

References:

Sir Jagadis Chunder Bose—His Life and Speeches. Filiquarian Publishing. Madras: The Cambridge Press, Print.
"The Man who Found a Plant's Heart." *Literary Digest.* 2 Oct. 1926 : 46,50. Print.

Editor's Notes: Bose's name is spelled in various ways, depending on date and publication.

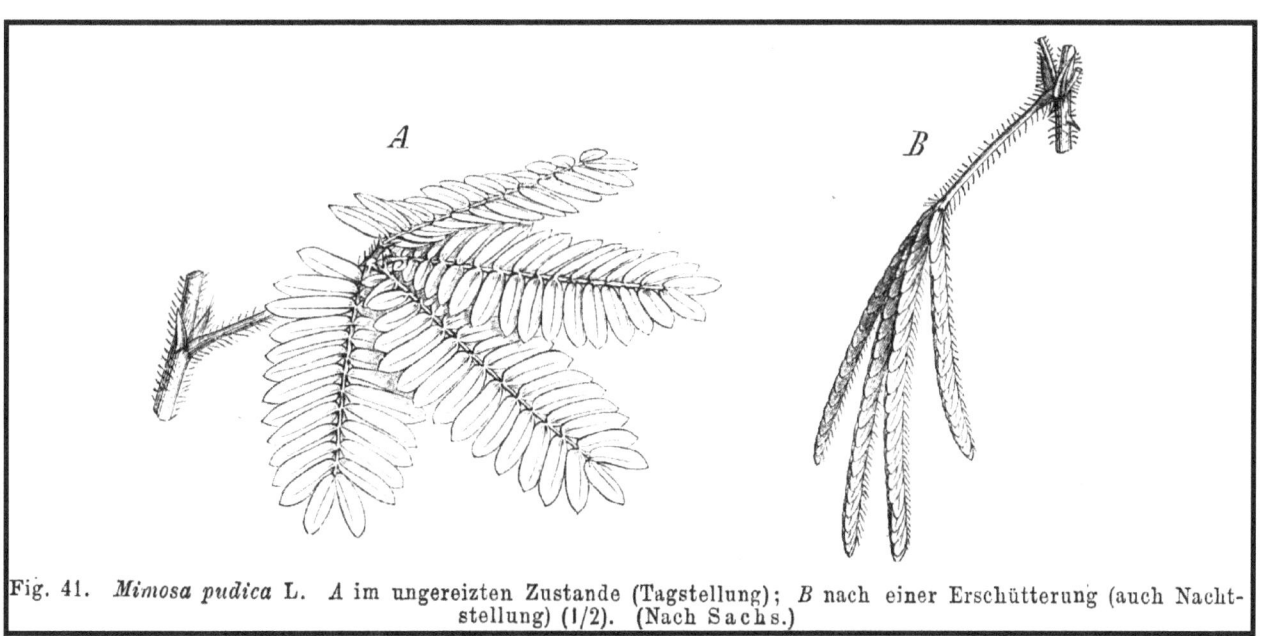

Fig. 41. *Mimosa pudica* L. *A* im ungereizten Zustande (Tagstellung); *B* nach einer Erschütterung (auch Nachtstellung) (1/2). (Nach Sachs.)

Mimosa pudica, by Paul Hermann Wilhelm Taubert (1862-1897) [Public domain], via Wikimedia Commons

Produce Party

by Mae Fayne & Angus Skillet

Woman Training Chicken, (photographer unknown), circa 1910, *Greenwoman* Collection

The Chicken Chronicles

by Sandra Knauf

s a typical modern American, I thought raising chickens seemed like a throw-back to the olden days, kind of like smoking your own hams or pounding your clothes on rocks down by the river. Still, it was my fantasy. I was already an avid, ecology-minded gardener, for three whole years, and it seemed the natural progression of things, going from cultivating plants to raising the animals that could provide their fertilizer. Ah, and what a picturesque fantasy! Chicken manure for the garden, fresh eggs, a sweet little henhouse with Martha Stewart charm in my very own urban backyard. It all began to be realized when I became friends with an elderly neighbor lady who raised bantam, or miniature breed, chickens. If she could do it, surely I could.

That winter Grandma Ruby and I hatched a plot. Ruby had two contraband roosters and four hens; we decided that come spring, when her hens "went broody" and began to "set" (got it in their heads they wanted to become mamas and began to stay on a nest of fertilized eggs) we'd pull a switcheroo. I'd transport the maternal chicken to a shed my husband Andy and I would convert into a hen house, along with a rooster for companionship, and then, in twenty-one short days, Voila!, we'd have adorable, peeping, baby chicks running about. Perfect rustic bliss.

Late spring came, and our plan went into action. One evening at dusk, I transported the chickens, in bushel baskets covered with worn bath towels, from Ruby's house to their recently renovated home. The chicken shack, as I called it, was clean, freshly painted, and nicely scented with pine shaving litter strewn on the newly-poured concrete floor. In the front, Andy had built a sturdy four-foot tall wood and wire fence around a small yard. Inside hung an old broomstick for a roost and three covered nesting boxes. A straw-filled box for the broody hen sat on the floor.

I gently placed the hen's toasty-warm eggs into the box. Then the birds, already named Deianeira and Hercules by our daughter, seven-year-old Zora, were released. They were handsome chickens, about one-fourth the size of regular ones, with cream-colored heads and golden bodies. Zora and her four-year-old sister, Lily, watched.

The Lilliputian rooster with long, curved tail feathers strutted his stuff, surveying his surroundings with a quick eye and elegant arrogance that could only come from a genuine cock-of-the-walk.

"He's a good-looking little guy, isn't he?" said Andy, smiling. I found this encouraging as Andy had not been thrilled with the scheme. To be honest, he often (though not coming out and actually saying it) left me with the feeling that he thought my idea was ill-conceived at the least and crazy at the most.

The hen, not in a cheerful mood about her abduction and relocation, ignored the egg-filled nest on the floor and flew to one of the wall boxes. That's okay, I thought, I'll just put the eggs under her there for now and then move her down to the floor when they're closer to hatching.

Deianeira pecked at me as I tried to gingerly slide the eggs under her. She then let out a screech of a curse and moved in a huff to an adjacent box. I understood perfectly: "I don't know who you are, but I don't like you!" After I filled the nest with her eggs she decided she'd get back on them after all. I felt a small cluck of triumph as we closed the door on the coop for the night.

The first dilemma came the next morning. Aware that we were harboring a rooster, I spent most of the night anxious, worrying about the racket he'd make in the morning. Sunrise crowing is not a city value, hence the five *hen* limit. My husband and I awoke at dawn and looked at each other. Silence. Great, I whispered, maybe he isn't going to crow at all! Ten minutes later, at exactly 5:20 A.M., Hercules began to announce the day. Now I didn't know if all bantams sounded like this, but this guy's crow was scratchy, hoarse, horrible, like someone with laryngitis, "UR...UR.... UR....UR.. Urrrrr...." It started out strong, then deteriorated to a deathbed gasp. Not like the movies. I closed my eyes. It's so loud! Maybe that'll be it, though.

Andy and I hunkered down in the sheets and listened. Hercules didn't stop, he sounded the dawn alarm every few minutes, and every time, I cringed. We didn't know what could be done about it (besides murder) so after lying there awhile, wondering if and when it would ever stop, we got up. I made coffee and waited for the neighbors to come over and string us up. So this was what mornings on the farm were like. "I didn't know it would be so bad," I said to Andy as I sipped my coffee, wincing

I made coffee and waited for the neighbors to come over and string us up. So this was what mornings on the farm were like.

at yet another cock-a-doodle-doo.

"I'm telling the neighbors it was your idea and I didn't have anything to do with it," replied my chivalrous mate. While we were both newly horrified every few minutes when we heard another fingernails-on-chalkboard salute, after a while we found ourselves grinning sort of perversely at each other at the wickedness we were up to.

Of course I'd decided at 5:20 A.M. that Hercules was history, but I had to wait before sneaking him back to Grandma Ruby's. We agreed I could bring him back, even though she said her neighbors actually liked hearing the roosters. I wondered at that now. A couple of hours later, after chasing the rooster around trying to catch him while Andy watched, laughing, and having the little guy

> Silkies are chickens whose feathers look like fur. You've heard of big hair; they have big fur. A sister-in-law calls them hippie chickens, but they look more like glam rock to me, the Ziggy Stardusts of chickens.

get a small wound on his comb in the process (the rooster, that is), I finally cornered him, threw a towel over him, and put him in Ruby's basket.

I returned to Grandma Ruby's with the basket on my hip and a guilty heart. I had not only chickened out on keeping the rooster, but had injured the beautiful, obnoxious bird. Ruby only assured me he'd be okay, asked how the hen was doing (fine, still on her nest) and graciously took him back.

Back at home, we commenced waiting for the eggs to hatch. During this time I tried to make friends with the hen. Several times a day I came in meekly, speaking in a soft and friendly tone, practically prostrating myself before the Queen of Eggs. I brought her the mixture of corn, millet, and other grains that they sell as scratch, plus a few treats, usually chopped up apples or greens. I tried to pet her. Every single time I came near she gave off outraged chicken vibes and pecked at my hand. She belonged to Grandma Ruby, no one else. She never left

the nest in my presence. I never saw her eat. Only once I witnessed her off the nest. I heard the frantic, "BAUK! BAUK! BAUK! BAUWWK!" and raced outside to her rescue. There she was, running around the fenced area, still "bawking," feathers ruffled. I couldn't find the source of her terror, and my appearance didn't calm her any. After a few minutes I shut her back in the coop to quiet her. I worried that she might not return to the nest, but she did.

After twenty-two days, Ruby and I became concerned about the unhappy, solitary, (crazed, in my opinion) hen—that she'd spend all that time on her great task, and, as Ruby put it "not have any babies." It was becoming clear that it would probably not happen. A few days before, I moved her nest to the floor in preparation for the big event. She became more furious than I imagined possible. She raised her hackles (all the feathers down her neck) and actually looked like a cobra. She began pecking at me vigorously, defending her eggs, and in the process broke one of them. There was no chick in it—just the shrunken, jelled remains of what once had been. I was surprised it didn't smell bad. The next day, I noticed an egg I accidentally left in the wall box when moving the clutch. I took it outside, nervously opened it, and found it, too, was empty. Both the hen and I were depressed. She'd failed as a mama and I'd failed as a chicken raiser.

The next day I called a feed store just south of our city. Now nearly July, I felt my time had been invested and I was determined to get chicks—one way or another. I inquired about ordering a couple of day-old bantam silkies as a back-up plan, in case the hatching did not occur. The feed store lady lent a sympathetic ear as I bemoaned my situation and said she'd call me back with a due date on ordering. Three days later the phone rang.

"Your Silkies are in," she said.

I caught my breath. "Oh, I didn't actually order them—I was just asking." Suddenly everything was happening too fast.

"I placed an order later that day and added a couple of silkies, in case your eggs didn't hatch. It's okay if you don't want them, someone else will."

"Wait," I said, suddenly all aflutter, "I do want them. I'll be down in a couple of hours."

My daughters, patiently expecting along with me all this time, were as happy as I was—we were finally going to get chicks. The week before I had shown them a picture of Silkies. They are not your average looking chicken. Originating from the Far East, they were first mentioned by the Italian explorer Marco Polo when he wrote about them during his travels to China in the thirteenth century. Silkies are chickens whose feathers look like fur. You've heard of big hair; they have big fur. A sister-in-law calls them hippie chickens, but they look more like glam rock to me, the Ziggy Stardusts of chickens. They look this way because normal feathers have barbules along the barbs (the individual branches off a feather) that hold the barbs together, sort of like velcro. Silkies lack these so their barbs go out in all directions, giving the fur effect. They're very fluffy, from their feet to their topknots, the feathers atop their heads. They come in black, white, and buff, have unique black-toned skin, and five toes, instead of the usual four. I thought they were very cool. Zora and Lily did not. When I asked if they'd like to have that type of chicken, they exclaimed in unison, "No! Those chickens look weird!" This burst my bubble, temporarily. Later, when I told my mom about their reaction, she said, "Don't worry. When they see them, they'll like them. Trust me."

Once at the warehouse-sized feed store, we were directed to the back where a big stainless steel horse trough held a couple hundred active, peeping chicks. A cornucopia of fluff danced before us— black chicks, white chicks, black and white, black and yellow, yellow, yellow with brown markings. There were bantams, about the size of a fifty-cent piece, and regular sized chicks more than twice that big. Baby chick acquisition greed swept over me. I quickly rationalized that since we were already there and the chicks cost less than three dollars apiece, it would be ridiculous to leave with just two. I asked the feed store lady if there were "extras."

Zora, who always astonishes me with her innate sense of style that I know does not come from my side of the family, nor from her father's as far as I can tell, fell in love at once with two big yellow chicks with brown speckles and stripes. They were full-size Araucanas. Araucanas are a South American breed that used to be advertised in the backs of old issues of Organic Gardening as the "Layers of Colored Easter Eggs." Martha Stewart raises them for their elegant turquoise blue and green shelled eggs. They are chic chicks. We were both disappointed to learn they were spoken for.

We decided to concentrate on bantams. The feed store owner scooped up my two white Silkies, who looked like fluffy white ordinary chicks except for their darker skin, and placed them in a small ventilated cardboard box. After some discussion, we settled on four more—two white and black chicks she called Golden Sebrights, a little black one with a yellow belly, and a yellow one that looked just like the kind you see in all the storybooks, except it had down-covered feet. With the latter two I forgot to ask the breed, and as bantams are too small to "sex" we didn't know how many would turn out to be hens and how many cockalorums.

On the drive home I felt giddy. The girls were too, as shown by their continual arguing over whose turn it was to hold the box. "Please be careful!" I pleaded repeatedly, my eyes darting to the rear view mirror. Amid the mania, I silently hoped that the mother hen would accept them so I wouldn't have to take care of them.

At home again we went to the girl's playroom, formerly a small sleeping porch on the back of the house. A cardboard box with a 60-watt light clamped onto one side for heat would be the chicks' temporary home. We gave them food and water. Since I read it was best to wait until dusk to try to sneak them under the hen, we had a few more hours to enjoy them. Over this time we played hostesses to everyone we could find who might be interested in seeing them—our next-door neighbors, the eleven-year-olds playing across the street, and a classmate of Zora's and her mother who happened by walking their dog. I figured if the hen accepted them we wouldn't be allowed close contact, so we indulged to the fullest.

Courtesy of U. S. Dept. of Agriculture

GLOSSARY CHART GIVING THE NAMES OF VARIOUS SECTIONS OF MALE FOWL

At dusk I cuddled a Sebright chick next to me and took it into the hen house. The hen eyed me with her usual dislike. As I nervously slipped the fully alert chick under her she reacted immediately. But it was not with innate love towards a new life. Instead she turned and began pecking vigorously at the chick—at its head. I screamed in horror and grabbed him. She screamed. We screamed in unison. For several seconds, chaos reigned in the darkened coop. The whole scene would have been highly comical if it wasn't so heartbreaking.

The next day Grandma Ruby told me I should have taken some of her eggs away first, but by then it was too late. There was no way I'd try again and risk getting one

> I recalled reading somewhere that the skeletal structure of chickens was very much like some of the meat-eating dinosaurs, and it wasn't hard to imagine little Velociraptors lurking under the fluff.

of the chicks killed. I'd already decided to raise them myself and she could hatch hers, if she had any, and we'd deal with it that way. After a few more days, though, I felt certain it wasn't going to happen with the hen. After telling Ruby I thought it best to bring her back, that I was pretty sure the eggs were not going to hatch, she agreed and asked me to first put them into a pan full of water to make sure. If they floated there were no chicks. They all floated.

With a heavy heart I returned the hen to Ruby. She had wanted me to keep her, as a gift, as a sort of living bond between the two of us in our mutual hobby. She wanted to share with us the sight of a mother hen being trailed by a group of rowdy little peepers. "I don't know why I like chickens so much," she'd declared on several occasions. Once she confided that her husband, who passed away seventeen years earlier, didn't share her fondness, and never wanted her to raise chickens. "After he died," she said, a determined expression settling over her beautifully wizened face, "one of the first things I did was buy some chickens."

The girls named the chicks within the first hour of their arrival—the Sebrights became Jessica and Suzie, the silkies Jane and Zelda, the little black one Julianna, and the yellow chick, Kayley.

"Great names for roosters," I said. We wouldn't know their actual gender for about six weeks, when the males were supposed to begin their first attempts at cock-a-doodle-doo-ing.

I admit that at first I was just a teensy bit anxious taking care of the babies. The temperature in the box had to be regulated—about ninety-five degrees the first week, dropping about five degrees weekly for about a month until they feathered out. I monitored the temperature daily, and fussed with the position of the light—each time I entered the room, which was often. I checked on them twice each night before I went to bed. I worried whether they'd have retina damage due to the constant illumination. I read about baby chick diseases and learned about something called "pasting up"—a condition in which runny droppings get stuck to their bottoms, causing elimination problems. So with a bit of tissue I pulled dried baby-chick poop off their butts. I can't believe I'm wiping chicken's asses! I thought. I had metamorphosed into their mother.

Peeking into the room during the day, I continually spied Lily with little black Julianna in her small, chubby hands. "Put that chick down and go wash your hands!" I said over and over. They had a lot of leeway to play with them, but with no admonishments they would undoubtedly try to take them into the bath with them. Already I caught them putting them in the dollhouse cars (they said the chicks looked out the windows), the dollhouse motorcycle, and in and on top of the dollhouse. They asked if they could take them out to the swing set. My biggest fear was that one of the chicks would accidentally be killed, ruining the whole experience and no doubt creating fodder for future therapy sessions.

Soon Zora and I began digging worms for their breakfast. We all gathered around the box, and one of us would dangle a wiggler until a chick grabbed it ran around the box—the others peeping excitedly in hot pursuit. Zora gave them voices. "No, Julianna, you can't have it," she'd have Suzie say, "It's my worm, it's mine! It's mine!" The girls, laughing uncontrollably, squealed as the chicks raced round and round. Zora exclaimed protectively when her favorite chick got a worm and the others tried to take it away. "Stay away! It's Kayley's! No!" She'd block the others off with her hands and I'd say "Don't!" We'd all gross out when one would have a long worm almost swallowed and another would pull on what was still hanging out of its mouth.

Then we discovered we could buy live crickets at the pet store. We'd buy a dozen or two at a time and dump the contents of the plastic bags into the box. The chicks would be on them with lightning speed. I recalled reading somewhere that the skeletal structure of chickens was very much like some of the meat-eating dinosaurs, and it wasn't hard to imagine little Velociraptors lurking under the fluff. The girls and I, accused of being bloodthirsty in our enthusiasm by Andy, knew we were just doing what any good mother hens would do.

They grew rapidly. Like Grandma Ruby said, it was almost like watching popcorn. Halfway through third week the Sebrights sported fully feathered wings, Kayley had a tiny comb and a few snow-white wing and leg feathers, Julianna had black tail feathers, distinct but tiny, sticking straight up, and the Silkies' down was even fluffier, especially on their large blackish-grey feet. When I found one of the Sebrights perched up on top of the box one morning, I knew it was time to take them to their outdoor home.

At first I kept a light on near one corner of the chicken shack because summer nights are chilly in Colorado and the chicks were not totally feathered out. As in their box indoors, they piled up to sleep, snuggling under the light. Within a couple of days, however, Julianna and one of the Sebrights started to roost away from the crowd. One night, after a couple of weeks, I turned the light off. The terrified peeping that ensued alarmed me. I then realized how tenaciously they clung to the warmth- and light-giving bulb. They would have to be weaned from Mother Illumination. I first lowered the wattage to forty for a few days, and then I actually made a trip to the grocery store and spent over three dollars on a twelve-watt nightlight bulb for chickens who were afraid of the dark.

They were spoiled in so many ways. We brought them table scraps and other treats on a daily basis and found out their absolute favorite (non-living) foods were corn on the cob, cantaloupe, and homemade split pea soup. They grabbed bits of ham from the soup and ran around covetously like they had with the crickets and worms. The girls and I began catching grasshoppers for them and discovered there were five different species living in our backyard. I showed them how to distinguish grasshoppers in the nymph and adult (with wings) stages.

We checked out books on chickens and found out our Sebrights were not Golden, but Silver. According to the illustration, almost every feather on their bodies, wings and tails would become a bright white, edged completely around in gloss black. The body shape would become sleek, like other birds, not rounded like most poultry breeds. The homeliest of the chicks, as they matured their slight builds and distinctly patterned feathering began to take on an elegant, even aristocratic, appearance. We learned they were a breed developed over thirty-some years by Sir John Sebright of England in the early 1800's.

> We read that Cochin chickens, originating from China, were the cause of an episode of "poultry-mania" in England in 1845. . . . Nearly overnight many Victorian yuppies longed to own one, and before the mania died down, some paid up to the equivalent of more than an average worker's yearly pay for a single "Shanghai Fowl."

The birds were remarkable in the poultry world for the fact that the male and female had the same feathering, shape, and coloring. However, we soon noticed that one of them was definitely growing a more pronounced comb and wattles—we had one of each sex.

Right from the beginning with the Silkies, Jane (my personal darling) was bigger than Zelda. But it was three months before there was enough distinction in his wattles and comb to declare Jane a John since Silkies also have near-identical plumage. The breed is prized for its gentleness and broodiness, and the hens are often used commercially to hatch eggs, especially pheasant eggs. In my reading I learned that broodiness, the desire to set on a clutch of eggs, to become a mother, had almost been bred out of many modern breeds of fowl.

Lily's Julianna, with "her" tail feathers growing more pronounced every day (Grandma Ruby's own foolproof way of determining a male), was also a he. Julianna was a

Black Rosecomb, a breed named for their unique combs. It lies low on their heads, is square in front, terminates to a pointed spike at the back, and is covered with small bumps. Julianna's comb and wattles were vivid red, and he sported white disk-shaped "earlobes," part of the rooster's dangly parts, as I called them, below the ear holes. His earlobes were perfectly round, enamel white, and added a jaunty, pirate-like air to his already cocky countenance. With lustrous green-black feathers, including long, arching tail feathers, he was handsome, and knew it. He was the first to crow. Lily renamed him Garrett.

Zora's bird also turned out to be a cockerel, though she remained in denial for a long time. As snow-white feathers on his rounded body and large orange feet began to replace the down, we soon I.D.'d him as a Cochin, of the bantam variety once known as Pekin. We read that Cochin chickens, originating from China, were the cause of an episode of "poultry-mania" in England in 1845. Presented as gifts to Queen Victoria from that exotic land, the public was quite taken with the breed's beauty, size, and gentle nature. Nearly overnight many Victorian yuppies longed to own one, and before the mania died down, some paid up to the equivalent of more than an average worker's yearly pay for a single "Shanghai Fowl." Kayley, like the description, was sweet-tempered and could be scooped up without fuss by simply bending over and sliding a hand or two under his soft breast. When he began to crow his voice was deep and unobtrusive, but also somewhat fit the (obviously exaggerated) description of Queen Victoria's birds who were said to "roar like lions."

So we ended up with only two hens and four cocks. Their crowing was not yet a problem, but we knew we probably wouldn't be able to keep them, though I told the girls we would for as long as possible. As the days passed, though, I began to hope that maybe we would be able to keep them until next spring and try for chicks again—Sebright and Silkies, and maybe a few hybrids. I was amazed to find out that most of our neighbors had been totally oblivious to the "Morn of Grandma Ruby's Rooster." I let them know what we were up to and asked them to tell me if the roosters became a nuisance.

For about six weeks we basked in perfect poultry happiness. Then one morning when I went to feed them, I found a cat crouched on one of the fence posts of the chicken yard. The birds were huddled in a corner, terrified. I shooed the cat and counted them—one was missing. My heart raced as I frantically searched the backyard. Nothing. I searched the alley, thinking that perhaps the cat took one over via the tree she came across. Still nothing. Zora came out and I calmly told her what happened, and that the female Sebright was gone.

We looked some more and as I neared the girls' inflatable three-foot-deep swimming pool I spotted her—floating, wings spread wide, eyes closed, her graceful neck resting motionless on top of the water. In a low voice I said, "Oh, Zora. I found her." Zora came over and we stood there, looking, fighting back tears. I went into the house to find something to pick her up with and Lily followed me out. It then occurred to me there was no reason I should be squeamish to touch her—I *knew* her. I lifted her out and placed her tenderly on the paper towel. The girls petted her. There were no signs of injury. Apparently the cat had frightened her into flying over the four-foot fence and into the pool.

We buried the Sebright near a semi-circle of small Siberian Elms the girls used for their outdoor "castle" area. I gathered smooth, pretty rocks to cover the grave and Zora found a red and white plastic Fisher Price farm set chicken to perch on top. A few minutes later she added part of a small, broken crystal sphere from the kitchen windowsill's odds and ends.

"I got this because Jessica liked shiny things," she explained. We gathered around the grave on our knees and I said a few words about Jessica's sweetness and goodness, how we all loved her and would miss her very much. Privately, I also felt disappointment at losing our male Sebright's mate and fully half our hen population. There would be no Sebright chicks next spring.

It never occurred to me that the pool was a danger. Grandma Ruby cautioned me about the four-foot fence ("Oh, they'll be able to get over that pretty soon," she said on her first visit) but I hadn't been very concerned. We had a six foot fence around the yard and secured the chickens in their coop each night. Besides, Grandma Ruby's chickens ranged her yard freely among her young cat Tweety, two miniature poodles, and various neighborhood felines (her ninety-some-year-old neighbor next door had thirteen). The only problems she'd experienced had been a marauding raccoon who killed a rooster the year before, and the time some obviously psychotic teenage boys abducted and murdered another, years earlier.

We had our own pet carnivores, but I'd never seen our cat, Merlin, a seventeen-year-old bag o' bones Siamese, hunt for anything other than a good place to nap. He showed absolutely no recognition that a flock of chickens had invaded his turf. Our fourteen-year-old black Labrador Retriever, Cato, was not only a creampuff, but he'd been blind in one eye since age two, when he was kicked by a horse, and was now nearly blind in the other from a cataract. He sometimes stood at the chicken fence, on now unsteady legs, and barked a few times, tail wagging. I imagined he saw blurs of chickens and surely smelled them and was making the canine assertion that he had some authority around here yet. Our only potential problem was Alice, the one-and-half-year-old Dalma-

tian we adopted the summer before. A spotted hell-on-four-paws—she was my outlaw shrub pruner the winter before—we nonetheless adored her. Alice menaced an injured wild bird early that spring, but only by bouncing around and barking. She never tried to hurt it. Knowing her potential for frolicking destruction, however, I kept close tabs on her.

When Andy came home from work I told him about the ordeal we'd been through and that we had to build a covered run the next day, on Saturday. After a morning of almost non-stop nagging on my part, we started the project. It took us only about three hours of constant bickering to put it together. I mixed the concrete for the fence posts and stapled the chicken wire and Andy cut and assembled the posts and rails.

The very next Saturday Alice dug under the run. The chickens escaped and again I ran around, heart racing, hunting and gathering. This time I found only three. The other Sebright was missing, as was Zelda, the female Silkie. Finding evidence of Alice's digging at the wire fence surrounding the vegetable garden, right next to the chicken shack, I investigated there. Sitting very still in a patch of grass was the Sebright. I took him into the house and examined him, discovering some minor scratches under a wing and a scrape on the lower right leg. He had apparently injured himself trying to escape Alice by squeezing under a low spot in the fence.

Vehicle-less, I phoned our veterinarian. Dr. Westrich told me that if I couldn't get in I should clean the wounds with hydrogen peroxide, keep the bird in a quiet place, and watch him. He also said that if the other one hadn't been found yet it probably meant that she wouldn't be found alive.

I made a box for the male Sebright named Suzie in the girl's playroom and went to search for Zelda again. I found her immediately—alive and well! She had been hiding out on the other side of the enclosed run—between it and a bale of straw. I spotted her as she ventured out into the open, peeping frantically to her coop-mates on the other side. I quietly thanked whoever was in charge of her safety for having mercy on me as well.

Early the next morning I found the Sebright hopping around his box. I picked him up for a minute and murmured consolingly to him, and when I left he made loud, distressed peeps. I comforted him again, and again he cried out when I left. The third time I went in he was perched on top of the box on his good leg. Maybe he would be okay outside with his buddies, I thought, it was apparent he would be miserable inside alone. In the chicken shack, his brothers and sister, noisy and excited, gathered around him, but he was hopping around so pitifully I changed my mind about leaving him. He needed rest. As I walked away from the other chickens with Suzie pressed against my breast, he began to protest—loudly and incessantly. With a nagging conscience, I returned him to his flock.

The next couple of days he seemed to be okay except for the leg—I could tell it was causing him pain. As the other chickens filed out of the coop into the garden to scratch for bugs and eat young weeds he protested loudly, then reluctantly hopped along behind them. Otherwise he ate, drank, and rested normally. I checked twice daily for signs of infection and found none.

On the third day I noticed the bottom of his injured leg was swollen. I called Dr. Westrich. Though he didn't treat birds, he agreed to check him out that afternoon. I figured the bird's leg was infected and that it would be drained and the doctor would put him on antibiotics. I wasn't really worried, and thought it would be an educational experience for the girls.

A friend of the girls' was spending the day with us and her mother said she could come along. As I carried the basket holding Suzie into the veterinarian's office, three little girls dressed up in tea party clothes—long colorful dresses, shawls, rhinestone jewelry, and parasols—traipsed behind me.

In the examining room, we gathered around Dr. Westrich as he gently lifted the bird from the basket, speaking to him softly and reassuringly. He examined him for only a few moments before pointing out the area above the swelling. "Do you see here, where the leg bends?" he said. "If you compare it with the other leg, you can see it shouldn't do that. It's broken."

My heart sank.

"And his foot doesn't have the healthy pink color that the other has. That shows that the area is not getting

> It felt like I was co-starring in the absolute worst, most melodramatic soap opera of all time—and I could not escape—the scene had to play out.

circulation."

"So it's getting *gangrene*?" I asked, completely horrfied.

"It looks like that's probably what's happening."

I asked if it could be amputated and he said he thought it could. He told me he thought the chicken would eventually be able to get around like other animal amputees, but that he didn't do surgery on birds. He said he'd call a doctor he knew, see what he thought, and try to set up an appointment.

The children had been silently taking in the unfolding drama. Zora now spoke. "Do we have to watch the other doctor do that?"

"God no!" I blurted.

The doctor, father of six grown children of his own, smiled at me sympathetically.

We waited at the front desk.

After a few minutes Dr. Westrich came back out and carefully explained, "I spoke with Dr. Abernathy. He said that in the case of amputations, the birds eventually develop a disease, an arthritic condition in the other leg, that ultimately debilitates them."

"So there's nothing that can be done?" I asked tearfully.

"You could go ahead with the amputation," he said, "but I wouldn't recommend it."

"We'd be putting off the inevitable . . ." I paused, trying to find an escape route from reality. "Are you sure it would be the same for him," I asked, "since he's a miniature chicken? They only weigh about a fourth as much as a regular-sized bird."

"I'm afraid so."

"I can't imagine putting him through more than I already have."

"We can euthanize him here."

"I think that would probably be best," I said.

I looked over at the girls chatting happily near the waiting room's aquarium. I felt dread, devastation and a large measure of self-loathing.

"You can use the examining room to talk to them," said the doctor quietly.

Trying hard to hold on to what little composure I felt I had left, I called the girls back into the examining room. Crouched before them, tears brimming, I told them what had to be done.

Zora, in a consoling tone I'd never heard her use before said, "Okay, Mom."

Lily's eyes filled with tears for a few moments before asking, "Are we going to bury him next to Jessica?"

It felt like I was co-starring in the absolute worst, most melodramatic soap opera of all time—and I could not escape—the scene had to play out.

We went to say our good-byes to Suzie. Before taking him away, the doctor asked if we wanted the body to take home, or if they should dispose of it.

"Please do it here," I said. I knew I was copping out. The girls could probably handle it, but I could not. Not two pet burials in as many weeks, even if they were "just" chickens.

The doctor brought back the basket and left the room to begin the euthanasia. Taking out my checkbook and pen, I asked the receptionist for the bill.

"The doctor says there's no charge."

"You can't be serious. I have to pay you."

"He said not to charge you." She smiled. "So don't worry about it."

When I got home I found I had to make a decision. On one hand, I could not bear any more tragedies. If anything else happened, the chicken experiment was officially over. We were down to four chickens and three were male. And I wasn't sure how long we'd be keeping them. After a summer of work and dreams we had one hen. On the other hand, we'd gone this far—we'd built the covered run, I'd now laid cement blocks around the parameter so the damn dog (I'd cursed her bitterly when we returned home that day) couldn't dig under it. I had nearly twenty-five pounds of feed, plus all the poultry paraphernalia—waterers and feeders, vitamins, a wire cage. The girls had bonded with their favorites, who were luckily still alive, and we'd taken a lot of pictures, documenting our "fun," including some wonderful ones of the girls holding the birds while wearing their tea-party clothes. I decided I'd give it one more try. But to make it worth-while, I needed to find a few replacement hens.

I browsed the local paper's Classifieds under "Farm Animals" and found no chickens for sale. Not profitable enough in the big city, I deduced. The County Fair had come and gone, and the only other places I knew of to buy poultry this time of year were the weekly livestock

U. S. Dept. of Agriculture
CROSS SECTION OF EGG CASE
Showing proper use of cup flats and fillers.

auction in the rural town of Calhan and the State Fair, now going on in the nearby city of Pueblo. Still quite the livestock novice, I was more than a little wary of buying at auction, so I called the fair. A helpful woman informed me they'd be selling chickens from the Junior Division Livestock Show in a couple of weeks.

On Friday of Labor Day weekend we set out at 9 A.M.. The trunk contained our outfitting: a wood-sided red wagon, two cages, and a basket, all made comfy with soft straw bedding. I had recovered from the previous tragedies and was looking forward to our hen quest, hoping to find my own objet d'desire, a Mille Fleur Booted Bantam that I'd seen in the chicken books. "Mille fleur" is French for thousand flowers, and "booted" refers to this breed's feathered legs. It's a fancy tan, black, and white bird, with feathers that are spangled, mottled, stippled pattern, or sometimes all three. Some of the tail feathers are two toned—tan on one side and black on the other, and most have white tips. Lily says they look like they have white polka dots. She decided she wanted to find a black chicken, to pair with Garrett, and Zora hoped to find either another Cochin or an Araucana.

At the fair, we found a parking spot near the entrance. The morning air was refreshing and the grounds quiet. Andy came along but we couldn't stay long because he had to return to work. After taking Zora and Lily on a quick run through the Arts and Crafts Building while Andy browsed the new trucks, we headed for the Small Livestock Building. We made a bee-line for the chickens, passing areas filled with pigeons, ducks, geese, turkeys, and rabbits. The sale had begun at 8 A.M., over a fourth of the cages were empty, and buyers milled about. The pressure was on.

Searching through cages of bantams, we found no Cochins or Araucanas, but I located a half dozen Mille Fleurs, and my decision was made. Lily fell in love with a black hen who wasn't for sale. Her second choice was a little Rhode Island Red. The hen seemed gentle and was handsome—her dark reddish-brown body embellished with black, lacy-topped tail feathers. An American girl, something new for our collection. I heartily approved. The Polish breed chickens, referred to as such even though they are thought to have originated in Belgium, caught my eye. They're the type with the big feathery topknots that resemble haute couture hats from the 1950's. I call them Dr. Seuss birds. Zora couldn't be persuaded into getting one; she declared them ugly.

She took her time selecting her perfect pullet—a medium-sized mixed breed. The young female was admittedly beautiful. Her body was graceful and tapered, like the Sebrights', but she was an Amazon. Her long neck displayed a multitude of thin, white, vertical feathers, setting off a body tastefully speckled in black and white. Her wing feathers were tipped white and her tail feathers black—the latter sticking up at a haughty angle. She had long, slate-blue legs, and her head featured sharp golden-brown eyes, a small red comb, and wattles. After being

> ## Towering over them all, she stretched her neck high and challenged them to question her authority. The girls screamed as she pecked at each and every one of the other chickens, including the males, when they were so insolent as to not bow down to her majesty.

around them a while, one can sense birds' personalities. Lily's Rhode Island Red and my Mille Fleur were easy to read—mellow. This bird was different. I detected an attitude of arrogance.

"Are you sure?" I asked Zora. "Why don't we look around one more time?"

"I want this one," she said.

I looked at the price on the cage. Twenty-five dollars. The hen I'd picked out was ten and Lily's was only six. But I knew there was no use trying to persuade Zora otherwise. She was a girl who knew what she wanted. Always had been. From birth.

As we were paying for the birds a photographer from the *Pueblo Chieftain* came up and asked if he could take a few pictures. Enthusiastic, but wary of having both Zora and Lily hold birds they were unfamiliar with at the same

time, I asked that he photograph Zora first. She happened to be wearing an ensemble—a black and white patterned dress with white collar and matching beret, both embellished with small, red cloth roses—that perfectly matched her new chicken. Then he photographed little Lily, whose hair needed brushing (though I didn't notice it at the time) and whose dark brown, blue, and black-checked dress probably made the Rhode Island Red nearly disappear on film.

As a final shot he posed them together. It became the final shot because Zora's bird got away and had to be chased down the long aisle of caged birds by a man with a net. While this took place, Andy returned. He'd been gone most of the time, visiting the hot tub display.

"What's going on?" he asked, eyeing the photographer.

"Oh, nothing. Just memorializing the occasion." I replied a bit bitchily. "This photographer asked if he could take pictures for the newspaper."

"Pictures for the paper?"

"Yeah, and you missed it."

We loaded the chickens into the cages and basket, then into our little red wagon. In the car the girls each happily held a caged bird, and I kept my chicken-in-a-basket with me in the front seat. It crossed my mind it would be very weird indeed if we got into an accident with three chickens riding with us inside the car. The girls chattered in the back, picking out names for their new pets and talking about being in the newspaper.

Lily exclaimed, "Now we're going to be famous. We won't have to go to school anymore!" We all laughed, but I had a sinking feeling. Knowledgeable about photography, I felt almost certain they would use Zora's picture. Either way, one of them would be disappointed, unless they used the one of them together, which I thought unlikely. I tried to broach the subject, but the girls were too jolly to consider anything negative.

Zora named her hen Aphrodite, after the Greek goddess of love and beauty. Lily's favorite goddess was Athena, the goddess of war and wisdom, so that became the Rhode Island Red's name, and they christened mine Hera, queen of the gods. (We'd been reading Greek mythology that summer). I loved their choices. One urban chicken farmer I knew of had named all her hens after country and western stars—Reba, Dolly, and so on, so I was pleased that the girls had picked up a theme of their own, without my help.

Since the chickens were all females, introducing them to the flock went off without a hitch. That night at dusk I slipped them through the door, and after a few clucks and rustlings everything went quiet.

The next day they began to get to know one another and re-establish the pecking order. I wasn't sure who was at the very top—it was either Zora's Kayley or Lily's Garrett—but Aphrodite asserted her dominance right away. Towering over them all, she stretched her neck high and challenged them to question her authority. The girls screamed as she pecked at each and every one of the other chickens, including the males, when they were so insolent as to not bow down to her majesty. After a few kicks and pecks sent back her way, however, she realized that the boys were supposed to be the leaders and she began to take on a more ladylike demeanor. And I stopped calling her Mighty Aphrodite, which irritated Zora. My bird, meek Hera, queen of all the gods and goddesses, immediately sunk to the absolute bottom of the order, and usually stayed several feet away from the other chickens. She was the last to approach the daily pan of tablescraps. Gentle and wise Athena took a middle rank.

The day after we brought them home, in late afternoon, Zora and Lily came running into the house. "We found an egg, we found an egg!" they yelled excitedly, holding the small, light brown gift from Athena. It was absolute magic to them, as if they'd discovered a jewel in the nesting box straw. I felt proud too—our very first egg.

I called the paper and found out that it was indeed Zora's picture they used in the Saturday edition. Lily was upset when I broke the news, but not as upset as when we finally got our copies of the paper in the mail the next week. There, on page 5A, we saw a full-color, six-inch by nine-inch picture of Zora holding Aphrodite. An accompanying article flashed the headline: "Lots of Cool Chicks at the Fair." Lily took one look and ran out of the house. We could hear her through the opened back door, at the swing set, crying as if her heart would break. Taking only a few seconds to marvel at the picture (we were expecting a small black and white) and how fun it all almost was, I went to try to comfort Lily.

She was swinging, and crying so hard her face was blotched red and white. "Why did they use Zora's and not mine? Everybody thinks Zora is better than me."

"That's not true, Lily. Her chicken just happened to show up better against her clothes. I'm sure that's why they used it. Please don't cry, honey."

I told her that no one in this whole city of Colorado Springs would even see the picture because you can't even buy a paper from Pueblo here. I told her that no one we knew would even know Zora was in the paper unless we showed them. I told her about other members of the family who'd been in the paper or on television for fun things and that her turn would surely come soon. Of course nothing I said was enough to soothe her. I learned

yet another lesson in motherhood. I did not expect Lily, who had always been very easy-going, to be so jealous, so traumatized. I felt incredibly stupid.

I wondered if a summer of ups and downs in the arena of backyard chicken raising had been worth the roller coaster ride after all.

My answer came several weeks later when Lily's preschool teacher asked if I could bring the bantys in for "Sharing Time." I decided to bring the three gentlest birds, Kayley, Jane, and, of course, our egg-layer Athena.

I prepared for the talk by gathering some feathers, boiling a few eggs (store-bought large and bantam for size comparison) and hauling out our globe so I could show the children where all chickens originated, the island of Java. As I lugged in the wooden cage holding Kayley and Athena, Lily looked up at me with sparkling eyes. The teacher told me I had five minutes. First I presented Jane, the Silkie, who was in a separate basket. I talked about his unique feathers and where his breed was from (the same place the Disney character Mulan was from!) I passed around feathers and eggs. Then, as I went to get Kayley, I asked Lily if she'd help with Athena. She deftly gathered up her little hen and was immediately surrounded by classmates who wanted to pet and hold her. It was Lily's turn in the spotlight.

In the car she told me how she had felt at show and tell. "Mom," she said, "I learned something today."

I looked in the rear-view mirror. "What's that, Sweetie?"

"That happiness can make tears come to your eyes."

"What?" I asked.

"I was so happy when I saw Athena I felt like crying—and then I couldn't stop smiling."

* * *

It had been one intense summer. If someone had told me what was going to happen in our little experiment—the profound highs and lows, the multitude of things to learn, to question, and to feel, over something so seemingly, inanely, simple—I wouldn't have believed it. Like an egg incubating under the warm down of its mother's bosom, the process of learning, of experiencing, took its own sweet time. I ended up reviewing a simple lesson: the most rewarding experiences in life are never, ever easy. And one more: If you are ever adventurous enough to find yourself doing something a little deviant, a little unexpected—say raising chickens in the city—you just might find you end up with something to crow about.

The first reviews are in!

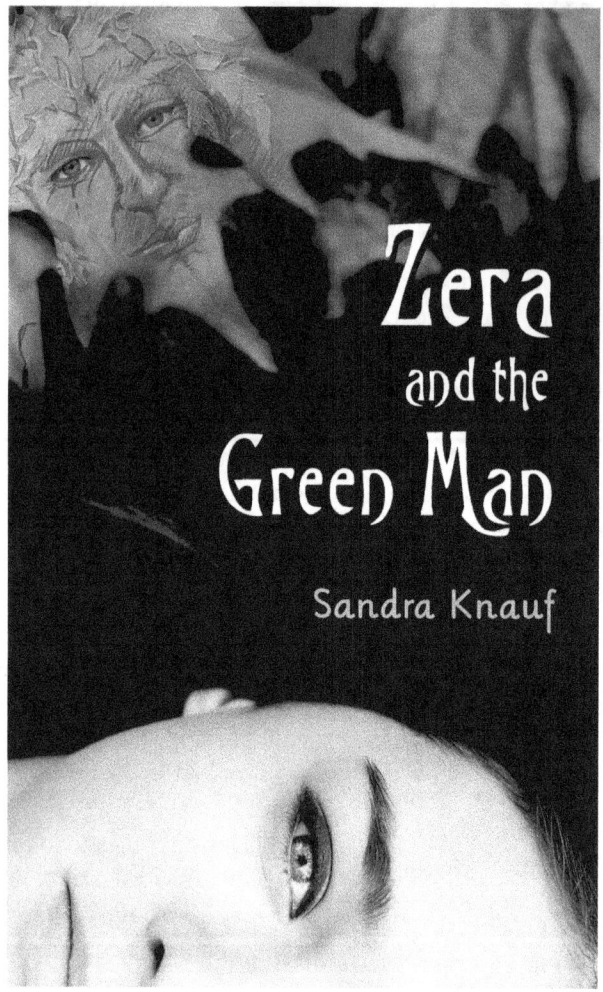

"An ambitious sci-fi novel that will charm eco-champions . . . "
–Kirkus Reviews

". . . . will leave readers hoping for a sequel."
–BlueInk Review

"The minor characters are exquisite: lively, entertaining, and complex."
–San Francisco Book Review

". . . one of those books that you'll want to pass on to your friends."
–Samantha Rivera for *Readers' Favorite* (five star review)

After the Cancún Summit
(an Abecedarian)

by Carolyne Wright

"The outcome wasn't enough to save the planet."
—Alden Meyer, Union of Concerned Scientists,
quoted in The Guardian, 12 December 2010

Atmospheric conditions over the greater global metropole indicate power
Brown-outs from sunrise all day until the hormone-heavy
Cows come home. Such solar overdrive! It
Dwarfs our efforts to maintain an
Elegant pretense before the assembled heads of state that
Fire won't consume the last few sticks of old-
Growth forest and leave this planet a bare beach ball from
Hell. Do ancient prophecies foretell that the people of
Israel will re-occupy their Old Testament kingdoms before Armageddon kicks in? No
Joke for Palestinians who cling to the only land they've ever
Known, if history and hermeneutics teach that they're the
Losers in this millennial chess game. Meanwhile,
Monster trawlers and cruise ships dispense a largesse of trash across
Nodes of the ocean's coordinates; bottom-dragging nets scoop up every last
Octopus and starfish and sea cucumber whose eggs
Pulsate with the next generation of by-catch, their
Queerly shaped progeny; and the Green Revolution yields
Rice bio-engineered to bankrupt family plots in Bangladesh.
                    How can human beings be so un-
Savvy? Where is the survival genome? You'd have to ascend
To the multi-billionaire tax bracket not to
Understand how we're spinning into a
Vortex of storm surges, colony collapse, and mercury yo-yoing
Wildly in the thermometers. Our committee will issue for your committee
Xeroxed images of extinct pigeons and woodpeckers and those flightless
Yellow Hawaiian lyre birds with liquid songs and glottal-stopped,
                    unpronounceable names. Soon,
Zoos may be the only refuge of all the species that used to roam the earth.

WE DIG PLANTS

LIVE Mondays at 3:30PM EST

Garden designers Carmen Devito & Alice Marcus Krieg of Groundworks Inc. delve into our human relationship with plants -- as food, medicine, fodder and as a source of beauty and inspiration. They bring the culture to horticulture and discuss such topics as botany how to, cultivation, horticultural history, garden design trends and all generally all things budding.

Check out this along with our more than 30+ live weekly shows and tons of great food news only on HeritageRadioNetwork.org

Leafing Through
a review of books, blogs, magazines . . .

by Cheryl Conklin & Joyce Deming

Grow the Good Life:
Why a Vegetable Garden Will
Make You Happy, Healthy,
Wealthy, and Wise
by Michelle Owens
(Rodale Press)

If you are fence-sitting as you contemplate leaping into vegetable gardening (or know someone who is) get your hands on a copy of *Grow the Good Life*. Once you do, set aside an afternoon, settle down with your favorite seasonal sip, and devour it. You will be elegantly persuaded to begin an activity that can have a positive impact on everything from global warming to your personal longevity: growing vegetables at (or very close to) home.

These are huge claims for a singular pastime, and they might seem totally implausible until you give this book a good read. An amateur gardener for twenty years, author Michele Owens writes from experience, considerable contact with other gardeners, and heaps of winter reading. In addition to persuading her readers that vegetable gardening is probably the one most powerful and tangible thing any person, family, or community can do to add quality to life, Owens claims it is also simple and easy.

Although I must say the claim of simplicity and ease may not hold as much sway as the plethora of other pithy arguments. Those qualities truly exist in the eye—

if not the lower back—of the beholder. While vegetable gardening is experiencing a remarkable resurgence in recent years, I'm not sure anything in this book will convince those who believe gardening is a chore. But it might, for many reasons, compel a person not already attracted to gardening to give it a try. To the uninitiated convert, Owens applies considerable intelligence and tempers her claim with sage practical advice. She offers this encouragement as well, "If you look at your own development as a gardener as an organic process, one where your ambitions grow as your experience does, you will be astonished at your powers."

With remarkable efficiency, dollops of acerbic wit, and downright affection, Owens elucidates topics as wide-ranging as the history and sociology of vegetable gardening in the United States since World War II and the beauty and beneficial challenges of gardening with kids.

"Beauty?" you might ask. Owens understands that many people refrain from converting sod to vegetables because they fear the aesthetic won't work in their urban or suburban setting. She knocks the legs out from under that stand. To her enormous credit, she also understands some would argue that beauty is a superfluous reason to create a vegetable garden. "There is nothing irrelevant whatsoever about the beauty of a vegetable garden," writes Owens, "even though a pretty one may well announce that its owner is a pleasure-loving fool."

Each chapter could stand on its own as a topical essay, eliminating barriers for the time-pinched reader who must consume it one bite at a time. My favorite is "The Soil: Why Dirt Isn't Dirty." I'm sure love of soil is a sign of the maturation of a gardener. After five decades of gardening (the last fifteen years or so in the semi-arid southwest), the preciousness, mystery, and preservation of soil is a passion of mine. Owens handles the subject with reverence and heart.

Cofounder of the widely popular blog "Garden Rant," Michele Owens has also penned articles for *O*,

The Oprah Magazine and *Organic Gardening*. Even those long-acquainted with the art and science of vegetable gardening will find delight, laughs, and great good sense to hurl at detractors in this full and highly readable book. —Cheryl Conklin

[Editor's Note: I must add that *Grow the Good Life* has been my number one favorite gardening book this year.]

How the Government Got in Your Backyard
by Jeff Gilman
and Eric Heberlig
(Timber Press)

During the height of gardening season, when faced with weeding, watering and the plethora of other garden-related chores, it's hard to think about books. Curling up with a cup of tea and a good book is more suited for long winter nights, unless that book is a mindless "beach read" and that tea is iced. But if you can pull yourself away from stalking slugs or tying up tomatoes, here are a couple of books worth your time. One is definitely heavy lifting; the other is eye candy with some great gardening advice thrown in. Happy reading!

What happens when you cross a horticulturalist with a political scientist? You get a well-documented introduction to the politics of organic food, alternative energy, genetic engineering, global warming, medical marijuana and other environmental topics. Jeff Gilman (the horticulturalist) and Eric Heberlig (the political scientist) have joined forces to write H*ow the Government Got in Your Backyard*. Don't let the title fool you. This is not some wackadoodle polemic about the evils of government. The book's subtitle provides more of an explanation: *Superweeds, Frankenfoods, Lawn Wars, and the (Nonpartisan) Truth about Environmental Policies.*

Nonpartisan is what Gilman and Heberlig are all about. In their book, the authors present the scientific facts and let you decide for yourself. They do give you some help, however. In addition to the basic science be-

hind each environmental issue, the authors present various policy options with left-wing and right-wing ratings ranging from one star (NO!) to five stars (Ideal Policy), as well as their own analysis. It's an interesting concept and if nothing else, you'll be introduced to both sides of a topic, not a bad way to get to the "truth." Who knows? You might even change your mind on a particular issue. This is definitely not "lite" reading, but worth the effort.

Now for some eye candy. Let's face it. Not everyone can chuck the 9-5 job, move to a homestead in the country, and grow their own food. Most people don't even want to. There are lots of benefits to urban living, and being in the city doesn't necessarily mean you can't garden. Reggie Solomon and Michael Nolan, authors of *I Garden: Urban Style*, have set out to show you how.

I Garden: Urban Style
by Reggie Solomon
and Michael Nolan
(Betterway Books)

In this lavishly illustrated book, Solomon and Nolan walk the neophyte gardener through every step of planning, planting and harvesting an urban garden. The first chapters are devoted to helping the reader figure out a gardening focus (food or flowers?), a gardening style (tried-and-true or freewheeling?), and a gardening plan (How much space and time do you really have?). These are critical steps for any gardener but especially important for the urban gardener whose time and space are often quite limited.

Later chapters cover container gardening, site preparation, buying or starting your own seedlings, commonly grown vegetables and garden maintenance. While the authors are experienced gardeners, they remember what it's like to be a novice and present the information in short, easy to digest pieces. This book is intended for the beginning gardener, but old timers will find useful information as well. I found the section on The 4-Hour Work Week enlightening, the recipes in Chapter 7 intriguing, and the resources in Chapter 8 quite helpful. Above all, the authors want gardening to be fun, something they call "Urban Garden Casual." I think they hit the mark. —Joyce Deming

Plant Whatever Brings You Joy by Kathryn Hall appeals to all readers interested in exploring the riches of a well examined life.

Author and gardening blogger Kathryn Hall is known worldwide for her successful blog *plantwhateverbringsyoujoy.com*, long one of the planet's top gardening blogs. Now Hall shares the life wisdom she has garnered in the garden in her book *Plant Whatever Brings You Joy: Blessed Wisdom from the Garden* by focusing on 52 lessons, each illustrated with heartful and poignant stories designed to spark the reader's wonder, awe and imagination. Book club folks will find this book a treasure.

"(HALL'S) WRITING IS A JOY TO READ: ELEGANT, FUN, AND DEFINITELY UNIQUE."—*Dig It! Magazine*

$19.95 | ISNB 978-0-9815570-0-7

Available on Amazon and Barnes & Noble as quality paperback, Kindle or Nook.
Visit www.plantwhateverbringsyoujoy.com
and www.facebook.com/plantwhateverbringsyoujoy for further information.

Flora's Forum

You are cordially invited to our garden party, *Greenwoman Magazine*'s group blog.
http://www.florasforum.com

"If you have a garden and a library, you have everything you need."
--Cicero

The Finished Book

Where is your book? The book that establishes your expertise and tells your story, the novel you always knew you would write. Where is it?

If you're like many would-be authors, your book exists in bits and pieces in old journals and desk drawers or on a computer disc. Maybe you're ahead of the pack and you work on your book fairly regularly, but deep down you think that you're not getting anywhere.

Call *The Finished Book*.

Together, we can make this the year your book is published. You can hold your book, turn your pages, and smell your ink sooner than you think.

We can step in anywhere in the process from the concept to the printed page.

The Finished Book will help your book become reality.

Please visit us at **TheFinishedBook.com** to learn more, or call Cheri at 719-235-3594.

Top Dressing
Never Underestimate the Power of One Tiny Seed

by Kathryn Hall

For anyone needing a prescription for faith and wonder I heartily recommend the following. Go to a nursery and buy a package of lobelia seeds. Any variety will do. Come home and *very* carefully open the package. (Make sure no breeze is blowing!) Look inside. Pour the seeds out in your hand and contemplate their minute size and then look at the picture on the front of the package. If you are not sufficiently moved, get some dirt, put it in a container, stick some seeds somewhere close to the top layer, place the container in the sun and water gently for ten days. As the delicate green begins to emerge and happy faced tiny purple and blue and white flowers begin to blossom allow yourself to contemplate the fact that the same forces of nature that govern the teeny lobelia seed govern *you*. Lobelia seeds, not unlike many others, are so small they would at first glance appear to have no value whatsoever! How could anything that tiny turn into anything anyone might be interested in? Yet given the right environ and nurturance the tiny seed grows to a healthy colorful plant that borders gardens and livens planters worldwide. If you were given the right sustenance, the corresponding water, earth, light and food, what might you become? There really is no difference. Anytime you forget your own value and worth, consider the size of the little lobelia seed and remember that you, yourself, contain a seed within that longs to come to fruition. That is what you are here for. That is your task and your destiny. What might you yield, dearest readers, under the right conditions? Take yourself there!

www.ingramcontent.com/pod-product-compliance
Lightning Source LLC
Chambersburg PA
CBHW080811120626
46556CB00009B/3283